WILLIAM
SPACE ANIMAL

Second impression published in 1968
This edition first published in 1967
by THE HAMLYN PUBLISHING GROUP LTD.,
THE CENTRE, FELTHAM,
MIDDLESEX, and printed by
Richard Clay (The Chaucer Press), Ltd.
Bungay, Suffolk, England

RICHMAL CROMPTON

WILLIAM AND THE SPACE ANIMAL

PAUL HAMLYN

CHAPTER I

William and the Space Animal

'I THINK those Space men look jolly dull in all the pictures I've seen of them,' said William, 'all covered up like tanks or washing machines so you can't see their faces prop'ly. It's a Space animal I want to see.'

'Gosh, yes!' said Ginger. 'Space animals ... Yes, I bet they'd be jolly int'restin'. Wonder what they look like.'

'P'raps they're a mixture of every sort of animal there is,' said William.

Ginger turned to look at Jumble, who was burrowing in the ditch, his fox terrier ears cocked, his spaniel nose quivering, his ragged collie tail waving wildly.

'*He*'d make a good Space animal,' he said.

'Yes, he's a jolly good mixture, is Jumble,' said William, surveying his pet proudly, 'but you can see he's meant to be a *dog*. I bet with a Space animal you wouldn't know what it was meant to be. Gosh! I wish we could find one.'

'P'raps Henry'll know somethin' about them,' said Ginger. The two were on their way to the old barn where they were to meet Henry and Douglas and plan the afternoon's activities. 'Henry gen'rally knows somethin' about everythin'.'

They strolled on down the road, enjoying the sunshine and the feeling of pleasant anticipation that a half-holiday brings with it, a glorious vacuum to be filled by fate with endless opportunities for adventure—opportunities · of which the Outlaws seldom failed to take advantage. Having

5

reached the window of the sweet shop, they stopped and examined the wares with frowning concentration.

'Creamy Whirls...' said William. 'They don't look bad.'

'They don't last any time,' said Ginger.

Two women and a man stood near them talking, and the conversations interwove themselves in an inconsequent fashion, neither group taking any notice of the other.

'We're on our way to Aunt Phoebe's birthday party. She's ninety so we simply must put in an appearance.'

'Barley Sugar Fishes.... Look more like tadpoles to me.'

'I've got Peter off to sleep in his cot and Billy's gone to Micky Fellows' fancy dress party, so everything should be all right.'

'Candy Kisses ... I wouldn't buy anythin' with a name like that, whatever it tasted like.'

'It's an Alice in Wonderland party and he's gone as the Gryphon.'

'Sherbert.... That doesn't last any time, either.'

'A friend lent us the costume and it's a bit big, but I wedged the head with paper to keep it steady and he *did* look rather sweet.'

'Mixed Fruit Drops.... We had those last time.'

'It's such a nuisance that it's Flossie's afternoon out—she's our maid, you know—but Mrs. Bruster's Milly is coming to baby-sit for us. She's only fourteen but so capable and sensible.'

'Orange Balls ... Jelly Babies ... Kid's stuff, Jelly Babies are.'

'Come along, darling. We mustn't miss the bus. Aunt Phoebe will be furious if we aren't there on time.'

'Giant Humbugs.'

'I feel a bit worried about having to come away before Milly actually arrives, but——'

'Yes, you can't go wrong with Giant Humbugs.'

'Flossie will hold the fort till she arrives, dear. Now come along.'

The group dispersed, leaving William and Ginger still weighing up the rival merits of the sweet shop's wares.

'How much money have you got?' said William at last.

'Twopence halfpenny and three farthings,' said Ginger. 'How much have you?'

'Threepence halfpenny an' a farthing. Gosh! That's sevenpence. What'll we buy besides Giant Humbugs?'

'Let's try Golden Nuggets.'

'No ... Chocolate Buttons. They've got diff'rent tastes inside.'

'No, they're too small.'

'All right. Let's toss for it.'

'All right.'

'Which penny shall we use?'

They considered their store carefully.

'Let's use this one,' said William. 'It looks as if it had a good sort of balance. I'll spin and you call. . . . Ready?'

'Heads!' shouted Ginger.

The penny soared through the air at a rakish angle, descended in the gutter and rolled down a grating with a distant 'plop!'

'Well, now *that's* gone,' said Ginger. 'You're a rotten spinner.'

'I'm not,' said William heatedly. 'Its balance wasn't right. I bet it was made by one of those coiners that get sent to prison.' He knelt down and, thrusting Jumble's inquisitive nose aside, peered through the bars of the grate into the murky depth below. 'If I could get it out I'd take it to the p'lice.'

'If we could get it out we could spend it,' said Ginger simply.

William gave a tug at the bars, then abandoned the attempt. Jumble remained there, gazing down through the bars, ears cocked, head on one side, uttering puzzled little growls.

'Well, we've still got sixpence,' said Ginger. 'What'll we buy?'

'Giant Humbugs an' Golden Nuggets. Some of the Chocolate Buttons are goin' mouldy an' I bet those are the ones he'd pick out for us.'

'All right.'

They entered the shop and asked for Giant Humbugs and Golden Nuggets . . . changed their minds when the Golden Nuggets were on the scales and asked for Lime Lollies . . . changed their minds when the Lime Lollies were on the scales and asked for Treacle Dabs . . . and were summarily ejected by the exasperated shopkeeper while in the act of changing their minds yet again and demanding Pineapple Appetisers.

They stopped outside the shop to examine their purchases. Jumble, attracted by the rustling of the paper packets, left his grating and leapt up at them excitedly, eager to claim his share.

'What did we get in the end?' said Ginger, who was in a justifiable state of confusion.

'Giant Humbugs an' Treacle Dabs,' said William. He examined the Treacle Dabs suspiciously. 'I don't b'lieve there's a whole two ounces here.'

'It went down,' said Ginger.

'I bet he's usin' false weights,' said William. 'I——'

Suddenly they saw Frankie Parker coming down the road. He took a paper packet from his pocket as he approached them, selected a sweet and popped it into his mouth.

'Hello,' he said. 'What have you been buying?'

'Giant Humbugs an' Treacle Dabs.'

'I got some Almond Titbits over at Marleigh,' said Frankie. 'They're jolly good. Why don't you go and buy some?'

'We've spent all our money,' said William.

Frankie brought another packet out of his pocket.

'I got some Nougat Squares, too,' he said. 'They're smashing.'

William and Ginger looked wistfully at the colourful slabs.

'Gosh! They look smashing,' agreed William.

'I'll do a swop,' said Frankie in a brisk business-like voice. 'I'll swop a Nougat Square for two of your Treacle Dabs, 'cause they're smaller, aren't they? an'. . . .'

Frankie was an expert swopper. He conducted negotiations with swiftness and finesse, and, when finally he set off again down the road, he left William and Ginger gazing thoughtfully at their diminished hoard.

'We don't seem to've got as much as what we started with,' said William.

Ginger's eyes had strayed to the shop window again.

'Gosh, William! Look! We never noticed them. Over in that corner. Liquorice pipes! Gosh! I wish we hadn't spent all that money.'

'Let's see if we can swop something for them,' said William, fired to emulation of Frankie's exploit. 'Come on in.'

The shopkeeper looked up at the clang of the bell and eyed the two customers suspiciously.

'Thought I'd got rid of you two,' he said.

'Well, listen,' said William breathlessly, opening his sticky paper packet. 'We want to swop two Almond Titbits an' a Nougat Square for two liquorice pipes. They come from Marleigh an' they're more int'restin' than anythin' you've got in your shop so you ought to be jolly grateful an'——'

He stopped. The shopkeeper was opening the flap of his counter and once again William and Ginger beat a hasty retreat to the road.

'Gosh, isn't he bad-tempered!' said William. 'He's one

of those British tradespeople my father was talkin' about las' night. They've got no imagination. They jus' say 'Take it or leave it.' They don't study the customer.'

'Well, let's start on the Giant Humbugs,' said Ginger. 'They'll last nearly till we've got to the old barn.'

They walked in comparative silence down the road, so much engrossed in the manipulation of the Giant Humbugs that at first they did not notice the woman who was signalling to them from a small cottage.

'You goin' through the village?' she said when at last they saw her signals and stopped at the door.

'Yeh,' said William indistinctly.

'Well, will you call at The Hawthorns and leave a message for me?'

There was a pause during which William tried to manoeuvre his Giant Humbug into a better position. Failing, he uttered a snort that signified assent.

'Well, tell 'em I'm sorry, but our Milly can't come baby-mindin' this afternoon. She's got a cold in 'er 'ead something chronic. Sneezin' fit to fetch the chimneys down, she is.'

William gave the joke the tribute of a guffaw that deposited his Giant Humbug on the whitened doorstep. He picked it up, brushed it on his sleeve and replaced it in his mouth.

'I jus' cleaned that,' said the woman indignantly. 'Now off you go an' give the message same as I told you an' no more of your monkey tricks!'

'All right, all right,' said William, managing to instil a hint of dignity into his muffled voice. 'C'm on, Ginger.'

The two proceeded down the road in silence for some minutes.

'Mine's gettin' near the end,' said William at last.

'So's mine.'

'I'm goin' to start chewin' now.'

'So'm I.'

They crunched with noisy enjoyment till suddenly Ginger stopped and pointed to a house. 'The Hawthorns. ... I say! Isn't that the house she gave us a message for? Let's go now an' give it an' get it over. Douglas an' Henry'll be wonderin' what's happened to us. We wasted *hours* in that sweet shop.'

'Yes,' agreed William sombrely. 'He didn't study the customer. He's jus' like the ones my father was talkin' about. He'll never attract overseas trade.'

'Well, come on,' said Ginger, going up to the front door and preparing to ring the bell.

But there was no need to ring the bell. The door flew open at their approach and a taut, trim girl, wearing hat and coat, her thin body a-quiver with impatience, stood on the threshold.

'Better late than never!' she snapped. 'Thought you was never comin'.' She surveyed them, her small sharp nose raised contemptuously. 'Well, I mus' say she's got queer ideas of baby-minders. Kid of a girl, it was, last time. Two kids of boys, this time. Well, it's none of my business an' I'm late enough as it is, so stand out of me way an' I'll be off!'

'Yes, but——' began William as the sinister implication of the words slowly dawned on him.

She interrupted him, thrusting him aside.

'Kid's asleep upstairs,' she said shortly. 'Other kid's out at a fancy-dress party, but someone's bringin' it back an' it can put itself to bed, more or less. There's sandwiches on a tray in the kitchen. Television's out of order. Radio's on the bookcase in the sitting-room. An' now it's all yours, so good-bye an' good luck.'

'Yes, but——' began William again.

The girl had hurried down the path to the gate and was running along the road to the bus stop.

'Hi!' shouted William, running after her. 'Hi! *Listen!*'

He was too late. A bus slowed down, the girl leapt upon

it and almost immediately it gained speed and was vanishing into the distance.

'Gosh!' he said. 'She's gone!'

'An' left us mindin' the baby,' said Ginger.

William swallowed the last fragment of his Giant Humbug with a gulp.

'Gosh!' he said again, in a voice so charged with emotion that it was little more than a whisper. 'She *can't* have!'

'Well, she has,' said Ginger. 'She said she had. She said, "It's all yours." She meant she'd left us mindin' the baby.'

'Well, what'll we do?' said William.

'Let's jus' take no notice an' go on to the old barn.'

'No, we can't do that,' said William slowly. Hidden deep beneath the lawlessness of William's composition was a sense of responsibility—erratic and unreliable and functioning intermittently, but still, in its fashion, a sense of responsibility—and occasionally it surprised even William by asserting itself in a crisis. 'We can't jus' go off an' do that. We can't jus' leave it. . . . Well, let's go in an' have a look, anyway.'

They returned to the house and entered by the front door that Flossie had left open. They looked into a pleasant sitting-room and went through to the kitchen where they found a tray of sandwiches and biscuits on the table. In silence and by tacit consent they divided these and disposed of them in a few capacious mouthfuls. Jumble found a rubbish pail beneath the sink and, overturning it with a skill born of long practice, set to work on some bacon rinds and a couple of cold potatoes.

Then they went into the sitting-room and turned on the radio.

'The Devonian fauna is intermediate in character between the Silurian and the Carboniferous . . .' a cultured, resonant voice informed them.

They turned off the radio and went out of the sitting-room.

12

'She said it was upstairs,' said William, standing uncertainly at the foot of the staircase. 'We'd better go an' have a look at it.'

Slowly and a little apprehensively, they climbed the staircase and entered the front bedroom.

In a cot against the wall, a rosy, curly-haired baby lay sleeping beneath a pale blue coverlet heavily bedecked with white rabbits.

William stood, gazing down at it.

'Looks quite a sensible one,' he said critically. 'It isn't yelling, anyway.'

'It might start any minute,' said Ginger nervously. 'Come on. Let's leave it. It's all right. Let's go to the old barn an' leave it.'

'No, we can't do that,' said William again. 'There's lors against leavin' babies alone in houses. They get kidnapped.' His drooping spirits rose. 'Gosh! It'd be smashin' if a kidnapper came to try. I bet we could fix him all right. We could start throwin' things at him before he got to the top of the stairs. I could throw water down on him out of the bathroom. I could hurl boulders down on him if I could find any. I've always wanted to hurl boulders down on someone.' He opened a cupboard and looked into it. 'There's a suitcase here that'd make a jolly good boulder.'

Ginger stood at the window gazing disconsolately up and down the empty road.

'Well, there aren't even any kidnappers comin',' he said. 'How long have we got to stay like this?'

William closed the cupboard.

'Till someone comes back,' he said.

'It's goin' to be an awful waste of time,' grumbled Ginger. 'Jus' lookin' at a baby for hours an' *hours*. It's enough to drive anyone ravin' mad.'

'We could do it in turns,' said William thoughtfully. 'You could go to Henry an' Douglas at the old barn an' then come back an' then I could go an' then come back.'

'*That*'s not goin' to be much fun,' said Ginger.

'No, it isn't,' agreed William. He looked at the baby and a light broke suddenly over his frowning countenance. 'I *say*! I've got an idea.'

'What?'

'We could take it with us.'

'Gosh!' It was Ginger's turn to feel the stirrings of conscience. 'We can't do that, William.'

'Why not?' said William. 'We'd be mindin' it, wouldn't we? I don't see it makes any diff'rence whether we mind it here or in the old barn. Come to that,' (as usual, once William had conceived an idea, arguments in favour of it flocked into his mind) 'I think we *ought* to take it to the old barn. It'd get some fresh air if we took it to the old barn an' it's not gettin' any here.'

'The windows are open,' Ginger pointed out.

'Yes, but there isn't any wind blowin' fresh air through them. I bet this air's been here all day an' it mus' be jolly bad for the baby bein' in old air like this. I bet that's what real baby-minders do—take 'em out an' give 'em a bit of fresh air—an' I bet its mother'll be jolly grateful to us for takin' it out an' givin' it a bit of fresh air. Stands to reason she will.'

Ginger tried to find a flaw in this argument, then gave up the attempt and set himself to the discussion of ways and means.

'How're you goin' to get it there?' he said. He examined the cot. 'P'raps we could carry this bed thing between us. It doesn't look very heavy.'

'No, we'll jus' carry the baby,' said William. 'It's easy enough carryin' babies. I carried one of my aunt's once an' I didn't drop it. I nearly did but I caught it again. It's not like carryin' square things like boxes. They go into any sort of shape, babies do. They're jolly easy to carry.'

'We'll have to take somethin' to keep it warm,' said Ginger, eyeing the occupant of the cot with increased misgiving. 'I know they've got to be kept warm. They've got to be made into sort of *parcels* with warm stuff. I've seen 'em out in prams.'

'Oh, we'll manage that all right,' said William. He spoke airily, but something of his confidence ebbed as he looked down at his sleeping cargo. 'We've got to pick it up first of all.'

'How'll we do that?' said Ginger. 'Will you take its head an' me its feet?'

'No, I'll do it,' said William. His face was set and strained with resolve. 'I'll do it. I'll count one ... two ... three ... and then I'll do it.' He drew a deep breath. 'One ... two ... three. ...'

'Go!' said Ginger.

Making a desperate lunge, William dived into the cot and emerged with the baby. The baby opened blue eyes, gurgled contentedly, then nestled back against William's shoulder.

'Seems to like me,' said William with a bashful smile.

'Well, let's get it packed up,' said Ginger, taking an armful of blankets from the cot.

The baby showed surprising co-operation and docility, allowing blankets to be wrapped and poked and swathed about it with only an occasional grunt, settling back to sleep again finally in William's arms. He was evidently a philosophic baby with a knack of accommodating himself to circumstances.

'Well, now, come on,' said William, stepping carefully down the stairs with his burden.

Jumble, having completed his investigation of the rubbish pail, had joined them in the hall, leaping up to examine the new addition to the party.

'I don't know that we're doin' right, William,' said Ginger thoughtfully.

' 'Course we are,' said William, combating his own secret doubts. 'We're givin' it fresh air. Gosh! I dunno

15

what would have happened to it if we'd left it in that room with all that old air. It might have died of some disease.'

'Oh, well,' said Ginger, as usual resigning himself in advance to whatever complications the adventure might bring with it, 'I don't expect we could get it back in that bed like it was before now even if we tried, so we might as well go on with it. Shall we leave the front door closed or open?'

'Closed,' said William, adding virtuously. 'We've got to look after the house prop'ly as well as mind the baby. We're doin' it jolly well, so far, I think. I don't see why they shouldn't pay us a lot of money when they come back.'

'I bet they won't,' said Ginger.

'Have a dig in my pocket for Frankie's Almond Titbits,' said William. 'This baby takes both my arms. Gosh! It's heavier than you'd think.'

The baby had accommodated itself to William's vice-like clutch and was still sleeping peacefully.

They walked along the road, munching Almond Titbits and gazing with awed interest at their sleeping burden. There were few passers-by and such as passed paid scant attention to the sight of a small boy, carrying, presumably, an infant brother or sister.

Henry and Douglas were standing at the door of the old barn.

Their mouths dropped open in amazement as they saw the trio approaching.

'What on earth have you brought that for?' said Henry.

'We're mindin' it,' said William, 'an' we've brought it along for a bit of fresh air.' He hastened to forestall criticism by adopting a tone of amused superiority. 'Haven't you ever heard of givin' babies a bit of fresh air? Gosh! You mus' be ign'rant.'

'Yes, but what are we goin' to *do* with it?' demanded Henry.

'We'll look after it in turn,' said William. His eye wan-

16

dered round the barn and came to rest on Douglas, who stood in the background, gazing in a fascinated manner at the baby, his mouth still hanging open. 'Douglas can start.'

'No!' protested Douglas. 'I don't know anythin' about them. I——'

'You needn't,' said William. 'This one's all right. It jus' goes on sleepin'. . . . We'll share any money Ginger an' me get for mindin' it so you all ought to be jolly glad to help. Sit down on that box.' He pushed the feebly protesting Douglas down on to the ramshackle packing case and thrust the baby at him, arranging Douglas's arms and the baby's blankets with a ferocious scowl and an almost maternal precision. 'Keep it jus' like that an' it'll go on sleepin'. It does. . . .' He dived into his pocket, brought out the sticky paper packet of sweets, carefully selecting a Nougat Square and a Treacle Dab and laying them on the ground by Douglas's feet. 'You can be eatin' those an' we'll go out now an' we'll come back in turns to mind the baby.'

'Yes, but—*listen*!' wailed Douglas. 'I don't *want* to mind it. I don't know *how* to mind it. I——'

He was wailing to the empty air. William, Ginger, Henry and Jumble were already crossing the field in the direction of the woods.

'How did you get it?' said Henry in an aggrieved tone.

'Oh, never mind that ole baby,' said William carelessly. The problem of the baby had been solved, as he considered, to the satisfaction of everyone concerned and he dismissed it from his mind. 'What'll we do now?'

'Gosh! I thought you were never comin',' said Henry, still harping on his grievances. 'I was late myself 'cause of this aunt, but—well, I began to think that somethin' had happened to you.'

'Well, it had,' said William. 'What aunt?'

'An' ole aunt that came to lunch an' stayed talkin' an' talkin'.'

'What about?' said William, who took an ever-fresh

interest in his neighbours and their concerns. 'What was she like an' what did she talk about?'

'She was awful an' she talked about the power of thought,' said Henry gloomily. 'She b'lieves you can make things happen by thinkin' about 'em.'

William gave this a moment's frowning consideration.

'Well, you can't,' he said.

'She says you can. She'd been to a lecture by a man that *knew*. He'd been out to the East an' met Eastern people that *did* it. One of them lay on nails an' didn't feel it 'cause of this power of thought.'

'Well, I don't see any sense in lyin' on nails, anyway.' said Ginger. 'I'd as soon not do it as do it.'

'Yes, but they did *other* things. They jus' *thought* things an' they happened.'

'They mus' think jolly hard to make them axshully *happen*.'

'Well, I 'spect they did.'

'Might be worth tryin',' said William after a pause.

'How d'you mean?'

'This power of thought. Might be worth tryin' to do it.'

'But you don't know how to.'

'I bet I do,' said William. 'Well, if these Eastern people could do it, I bet I could. I'd think harder an' harder an' *harder* for minutes an' minutes an' *minutes* till I'd got this power of thought goin' then I'd wish.'

'What would you wish?' said Henry, impressed by William's earnestness.

William considered.

'I know!' he said at last. 'Ginger an' me were talkin' about it jus' now. I'd wish a Space animal to come. I'm sick of pictures of Space men. I want to see a Space animal.'

'I bet you won't. Not with jus' thinkin'.'

'All right. You wait an' see,' said William. 'I'm goin' to start now...' They had entered the wood and the path

18

'Gosh!' said William faintly. 'A Space animal!'

before them wound through the trees, then swerved sharply out of sight. 'I'm goin' to think hard till we get to that turn, then I'm goin' to wish. Now I'm goin' to start, so shut up.'

Walking on either side of William, Henry and Ginger watched his face with growing concern. It was set and scowling. The power of thought evidently precluded the function of breathing, for it turned pink, then red, then purple . . . the veins on his forehead became congested, his cheeks bulged.

'I say, stop it, William,' said Ginger anxiously. 'You're goin' to burst.'

William had reached the turn of the path. He stopped, let out his breath in a prolonged puff and gasped:

'I wish to see a Space animal.'

And then—through the undergrowth between the trees came a small green figure with green head, green wings, green body, green tail. It walked disconsolately and wailed as it walked.

'Gosh!' said William faintly. 'A Space animal!' The purple colour brought into his face by the process of thought had faded to an almost ashen hue. 'Gosh! I've *done* it.'

As if attracted by his voice, the creature turned and approached him. The wails died away to a whimpering.

'Good——' began William reassuringly and ended somewhat lamely, 'Space animal!' as he patted the green head.

Jumble, after a moment's doubt, had evidently decided to admit the newcomer into his large circle of friends and acquaintances and was leaping up in welcome, wagging his tail.

'Seems quite tame,' said William, 'an' Jumble likes it.'

'It's jolly int'restin',' said Ginger, walking round it. 'It's quite diff'rent from any animal we've got on the earth, isn't it?'

20

'Yes . . . it's got claws an' paws,' said William.

'An' wings.'

'An' ears an' a beak.'

'Funny sort of noise it makes,' said Henry as the wailing began again.

'Bit like a cat,' said Ginger.

'Or a hyena,' said William.

'Or a factory whistle,' said Ginger.

Then Henry asked the pertinent question.

'What are we goin' to do with it?'

'Y-yes,' said William, wrinkling his brows. 'Now we've brought it down from Mars or the moon or wherever it comes from we've got to treat it right.'

'We don't know what it eats,' said Ginger.

William brought out his sticky paper packet, carefully selected a Treacle Dab and offered it to the newcomer. The newcomer showed neither pleasure nor interest.

'I'll put it on the ground by it,' said William, placing the Treacle Dab on the ground by the visitor. 'It might be used to eatin' off the ground.'

Still the creature showed neither pleasure nor interest.

'It doesn't like it,' said William, picking up the Treacle Dab and replacing it in the packet.

'Well, we'll have to feed it,' said Ginger. 'We can't let it starve.'

'An' where'll we keep it?' said Henry.

'We could keep it a week in turns,' said William.

'Yes, an' everyone'll find out,' said Ginger. 'You can't keep a Space animal like that secret.'

'Wonder what they think's happened to it up in Mars or the moon,' said William. 'I s'pose it jus' disappeared.'

'Hope it doesn't start a Space war,' said Ginger, glancing anxiously up at the sky.

The Space animal was sitting on the ground, whimpering a little but obviously taking comfort from their presence.

'Grown-up people that find strange animals give them to the zoo,' said Henry.

'Yes, we could do that,' said William. 'We could give it to the zoo.'

'We don't know how to get it there,' objected Ginger. 'Anyway, we haven't any money to buy its ticket an' I 'spect they'd charge an awful lot of money for it on the railway.'

'There's the British Museum,' said Henry. 'People sometimes give things they find to the British Museum. . . .'

'Yes,' said William indignantly, 'an' it'd have a jolly dull time there with statchoos an' mummies an' things. No, it's not goin' to the British Museum.' Suddenly the light of an idea broke through the gloom of his countenance. '*Tell* you what!'

'Yes?' they chorused eagerly.

'We could take it to Emmett's animal shop an' sell it to him. It'd be all right there.'

'He wouldn't buy that insect collection you tried to sell him,' said Ginger.

'Well, he wasn't int'rested in insects,' said William. 'He'd be int'rested in a Space animal. Stands to reason. Anyone'd be int'rested in a Space animal. I bet he'd give us a jolly lot of money for it. An' he'll know what to feed it on an' if the zoo wants it they can come an' get it off him. Let's go there with it now.'

'All right,' agreed the others.

William took a paw of the Space animal in his hand.

'Come on, ole boy,' he said. 'Come on, ole Space animal.'

It grasped his hand trustingly and began to trot along beside him, the whimpers dying away to a murmur.

They went across the fields and along the main street of Hadley. Passers-by threw them amused and curious glances, but no one stopped or questioned them. Having arrived at Emmett's animal shop, they paused to look in at the window ... puppies, kittens, hamsters, rabbits, guinea pigs, tortoises, goldfish in bowls, birds in cages. . . .

'Look, he's got all sorts,' said William, 'an' they all seem jolly happy. I bet a Space animal'd settle down with 'em all right. He knows what to give 'em to eat an' I bet he'd know what to give a Space animal. He could try diff'rent sorts of animal food on it, anyway. An' it'll look jolly fine in the window there.'

'It's a bit big,' said Ginger, looking down at their exhibit.

'Well, he can keep it in the shop. He can keep it in a dog kennel. I bet he'll sell it for pounds an' *pounds* when people come to know about it. Gosh! It mus' be the only one in England. I bet the zoo'll want it as soon as they hear about it. I bet——'

'Well, come on in,' interrupted Henry, who was beginning to wear a faintly harassed air now that the affair was nearing its crisis.

William opened the shop door and entered, holding his charge by the paw, followed by Henry, Ginger and Jumble.

A vague-looking boy of about thirteen came forward.

'My uncle's jus' gone out,' he said in an adenoidal voice. 'He said if any customers came they was to wait an' he'd be back in a minute.'

'Well, we're in a hurry,' said William importantly. 'We've come to sell a Space animal.'

'A——?' The boy looked down at the small green figure and a spark of interest came into his impassive face. 'A— what did you say?'

'A Space animal,' reported William impatiently. 'Have you never heard of a Space animal? It's the only one in England an' it's jolly valu'ble. We're chargin' '—he drew a deep breath—'five pounds for it. I bet it's worth a hundred.'

'Or a thousand,' said Ginger.

'But we'd take less,' put in Henry hastily. 'We'd take ten shillings.'

'Or even five,' said William.

'We wouldn't mind two an' six,' said Ginger.

A loud wail came from the green head.

'That's the noise they make, Space animals,' said William. 'Well, what about it?'

The spark of interest had faded from the boy's impassive face.

'He said I'd not got to buy nothin',' he said. 'He said I was to tell customers he'd be back in a minute.'

'Well, look!' William's eyes had strayed to a shallow box of baby tortoises. 'We'll swop it for a baby tortoise. Gosh! Your uncle'll be jolly glad to find you've swopped a baby tortoise for a valu'ble Space animal. That's a *bargain*, that is.'

'I dunno . . .' said the boy doubtfully.

'He'll be *mad* with you if he comes back an' finds you've let a bargain like that go . . . a valu'ble Space animal for jus' a baby tortoise. If you'll let me have the baby tortoise you can have the Space animal now at once an' you'll prob'ly have made your fortune. You'll be *famous*. You'll have your picture in the *newspapers*. It's the only Space animal in the whole world, I tell you, an'——'

'Oh, all right,' said the boy, overwhelmed by the torrent of William's eloquence.

'Thanks,' said William.

He carefully selected a baby tortoise and slipped it into his pocket.

'There you are!' he said, giving the Space animal a gentle push towards its new owner.

At that moment the shop door opened and Mr Emmett appeared.

He eyed the customers without enthusiasm.

'What's all this?' he said.

'We've come to sell a Space animal,' said William. 'It's

worth hundreds of pounds but we'll take five.'

'Or ten shillings,' said Henry.

'Or two an' six,' said Ginger.

Another wail rose from the green head.

'That's the noise they make,' explained William again.

Mr. Emmett strode across the shop, took hold of the green head and wrenched it off, revealing a round, rosy face, scratched and tear-stained, which broke into a beam of delight when disclosed to view.

'I was a Gryphon an' I got stuck,' explained the Space animal. 'It got stuck on my head so it hurt me an' I couldn't see anything so I ran away an' I cried but it's all right now.'

'Gosh!' gasped William. 'It's not one, after all.'

Mr. Emmett's grim features did not relax.

'Clear out, the lot of you!' he said. 'Any more of your nonsense and——'

But already William was leading his band in disordered flight into the street. Jumble, who had stayed to secure a dog biscuit from an overflowing sack, brought up the rear. In the street they stopped and looked at each other. The small boy's face was still wreathed in smiles. He had picked up his head and was carrying it under his arm.

'I was stuck in it,' he explained again. 'He unstuck me. He was a kind man.'

'Well, you can go home now,' said William coldly. 'We've taken a lot of trouble over you all for nothing.'

'Can't go home,' said the child, with another engaging smile. 'Lost.'

'Well, you've been enough of a nuisance already,' said William sternly. He felt a natural resentment against the erstwhile Space animal. 'You've wasted hours an' *hours* of our time an' you can jolly well go away now.'

The boy beamed at him.

'I got stuck in it,' he said, evidently considering that his adventure had not been accorded its due meed of interest.

25

'I was a Gryphon an' I got stuck in it.'

'Oh, come on,' said William, turning to the others with an air of disgust.

They set off again across the fields. The small boy accompanied them, his face still wearing its all-embracing smile. Jumble trotted at his heels, every now and then leaping up at the Gryphon's head. Each time he did it, the small boy's laugh pealed out.

'Dog likes it,' he said delightedly. 'Look! Dog likes it.'

When they reached the wood the three Outlaws sat down beneath a tree to consider the situation. The small boy sat with them, still chuckling at Jumble's attempts to investigate the head.

'What's your name?' said William sternly.

The boy thought for a minute.

'Gryphon,' he said at last proudly.

'Do you live near here?'

'Yes.'

'Were you going home when we found you?'

'Yes.'

'Can't you say anything but "yes"?'

'Yes.'

'Well, say it.'

'Yes.'

Freed of the encumbrance of his head, he was a frolicsome child with a pronounced if crude sense of humour.

'Ask me some more,' he shouted. 'Ask me some more an' I'll say "yes".'

His merriment was infectious.

'You're an idiot, aren't you?' said Ginger.

'Yes,' chuckled the child.

'Do you have frog pie for tea?' said Henry.

'Yes.'

'Do you go to bed in the chimney?'

'Yes.'

The four of them rolled about in mirth. The small boy,

shouting with delight, turned a somersault backwards. Jumble took it as an invitation to a game of the rougher variety and sprang upon him, tearing with playful ferocity at the green suit in which he was enveloped. The boy's laughter and Jumble's mock growls rang out as piece after piece of the flimsy costume gave way before Jumble's onslaught. Feathers flew in all directions as he tore off the wings ... lengths of material and cardboard strewed the ground. He worried them and tossed them into the air, taking the laughter and applause as encouragement to further effort. Finally he set to work on the head, which had rolled to the foot of the tree, chewing, worrying, growling.

The small boy stood up, still chuckling with delight, but the delight of the Outlaws faded somewhat as they surveyed him. The Gryphon suit was now a mere frill round his plump waist. The upper part hung precariously from his shoulders.

'Gosh!' said William. 'What are you goin' to do now? Are you goin' home?'

'Yes,' said the boy, turning to set off among the trees.

'Do you know the way?' said William.

The boy's voice came from the distance, high-pitched with laughter.

'Yes,' it said.

'He wasn't a bad kid,' said Ginger, 'an' a real Space animal might have been a bit of a nuisance. I 'spect this power of thought gets a bit muddled. I mean, you wished for a Space animal an' it got you the nearest it could find. I mean, it got you somethin' that *looked* like a Space animal.'

But William wasn't listening. A dreamy expression had come into his face.

'Gosh!' he said. 'I've jus' remembered somethin'.'

'What?'

'That baby we're s'posed to be mindin'.' He stood up.

27

'We'd better be gettin' back to it.'

'It'll be all right,' Ginger reassured him. 'Douglas is with it.'

'Yes, but we said we'd go an' take our turns. He'll be gettin' mad with us. Come on.'

They set off briskly towards the old barn. It lay silent and peaceful in the sunshine.

'It's not started yelling yet, anyway,' said Henry. 'I knew ole Douglas'd manage all right.'

They reached the open doorway and looked into the dim recesses of the barn.

Douglas was there, turning over a heap of old sacks in the farther corner, his face wearing an expression of tense anxiety.

'Where's the baby?' said William.

'I don't know,' said Douglas. 'It's gone.'

'Gone!' echoed William. 'It couldn't have. It can't walk.'

'Well, it has,' said Douglas. 'You went on and on not comin' an' I couldn't think what'd happened to you an' I thought I'd jus' go as far as the end of the wood an' see if I could see you an' it seemed all right 'cause it was still asleep so I put it down on these sacks an' went to try'n find you an' I couldn't so I came back an'—it'd gone.' He continued to turn over the sacks with a distracted air. 'It isn't anywhere here at all. I've looked everywhere.'

'Gosh! *Now* you've done it!' said William, aghast.

'Losin' a baby! There's lors against it. I bet we'll all get put in prison.'

'But it couldn't walk,' protested Douglas.

'It may've started to walk while you were out. They *do* start to walk. It may've come over it quite sudden how to walk while you were out.'

'It may have crawled,' said Ginger. 'I've seen them crawling.'

'Well, anyway,' said William, 'let's go'n have a good

28

look through the woods 'case it's there. Gosh! Its mother'll be in an awful state.'

Its mother was not in an awful state. She was walking with her husband from the station discussing Aunt Phoebe's party in a placid, leisurely fashion.

'She's a dear old thing,' she said, 'and she was so glad to see us.'

'Yes,' agreed her husband. 'It was quite worth making the effort to go.'

'It was lucky we could get Milly to mind Peter and lucky that Billy was going to the party. He did look sweet in his Gryphon suit, didn't he?'

Mr. Clayton smiled.

'He looked the young ruffian he is,' he said.

'It'll be lovely to get home again and find Peter asleep in his cot and——'

'Mrs. Clayton!' called a voice behind them.

They turned to see Miss Milton hurrying along the road, her small face pursed in anxiety.

They stopped.

'What's the matter, Miss Milton?'

'Oh dear!' panted Miss Milton. 'Oh, dear! I'm in such a state I hardly know what to do. I've just found an abandoned baby in that old barn in the field.'

'An——?'

'An abandoned baby. I've been over to see some friends at Marleigh and I was coming home by the short cut across the fields and I just glanced in at the door of the barn and there I saw it—an abandoned baby.'

'What did you do?' said Mrs. Clayton.

'I picked it up and took it home,' said Miss Milton. 'I couldn't think of anything else to do. I couldn't leave it there abandoned to die of exposure, though it *had* a lot of blankets with it. Anyway, I brought it home and now I'm on my way to tell the police about it, but I'm feeling terribly worried because I've no one to leave it with and I've left it alone in the house tucked up on the settee and though it looks quite comfortable *anything* might happen to it.'

'Why didn't you bring it to our house?' said Mrs. Clayton. 'Go and fetch it and we'll look after it while you go to the police.' She smiled. 'We've got one baby, you know, and another wouldn't make much difference.'

'Oh, thank you so much,' said Miss Milton. 'What a good idea! That's a great relief. I'll fetch it now.'

She turned and scuttled off down the road.

'What an extraordinary thing!' said Mr. Clayton. 'Whoever would abandon a baby in a barn?'

'People do,' said Mrs. Clayton. 'You read about it in newspapers.... Well, the darling can share Peter's things till some arrangement has been made for him. He——' She stopped short. Another figure had appeared, hurrying—almost running—down the road towards them. 'Whoever's this? Why, it's Mrs. Monks.'

Mrs. Monks came up to them. Her face, like Miss Milton's, was pursed in anxiety.

'Oh, dear!' she said. 'I should so like your advice. I've just found a little lost boy.'

'A little——?'

'A little lost boy. I think he's one of that family of Hungarian acrobats who were performing at the circus at Hadley last week. They went this morning and must have left the child behind in the confusion. I didn't see them myself but I heard that they all wore little green frills and that's what he's wearing and the youngest was about four years old and he seems about that age. I asked him his name and he said something that sounded like Gaifon. A Hungarian name undoubtedly. I asked him if he was Hungarian and he said "Yes". I asked him if he was one of the family of acrobats and he said "Yes". I asked him if he was lost and he said "Yes". He seemed to understand Eng-

lish but not speak it much. Quite a cheerful little boy ...
but I must of course try to get into touch with his parents
at once.'

'Where is he now?' said Mrs. Clayton.

'That's what's worrying me. I took him home and made
him some bread and milk and then I thought I'd go and
tell the police. So much more satisfactory to do these
things personally. ... Besides, I can never hear what that
man at the police station says on the telephone. He has a
most indistinct voice. But I *am* a bit worried about leaving
the child alone in the house. I didn't want to take him
through the village in his acrobat costume and yet it's just
struck me that he might possibly wander out of the house
and get lost again ... I really don't know what to do.'

'Run back home and bring him along to our house,' said
Mrs. Clayton. 'We're going to have an extra baby anyway,
so an extra little boy won't make any difference. We'll keep
him happy and comfortable till they've made some
arrangement about sending him on to the circus.' She
turned to her husband with a smile. '*Four* children now,
darling, but I think we can cope.'

'Sure!' said Mr. Clayton.

He was the sort of man who takes things in his stride.

'Oh, that's splendid,' said Mrs. Monks. 'I'll run back
now and fetch him to you then I'll go and make my per-
sonal report to the police.'

She hurried back down the road and Mrs. and Mr. Clayton strolled on towards their house.

'I shall have to get busy with blankets and things for our
two little visitors,' said Mrs. Clayton. 'Fortunately I've got
heaps. Mother was so deliciously Victorian in stocking us
up with *dozens* of everything.'

'Well, there's something in it,' said Mr. Clayton.

He unlocked the door, and they entered the hall.

'Milly!' called Mrs. Clayton in a pleasant tone of greeting.

There was no answer.

'Milly!' called Mrs. Clayton, a note of anxiety replacing the pleasant note of greeting.

There was no answer.

'Milly!' she called again, a note of anguish replacing the anxiety.

'Milly!' called Mr. Clayton with a mixture of foreboding, bewilderment and male authority.

There was no answer.

Mrs. Clayton ran upstairs to the bedroom and stood for a few moments, paralysed by horror, gazing down at the empty cot.

'He's gone,' she screamed. 'Peter's gone!'

Mr. Clayton took the stairs three at a time and gazed aghast at the disordered sheets and coverlet.

'What on earth's happened?' he said.

'He's been kidnapped,' wailed Mrs. Clayton. 'They've taken him, blankets and all. They've *kidnapped* him.' She went into the next room and gave another scream. 'Billy's not here either. He should have been back from the party long ago.'

'Where's Milly?' said Mr. Clayton.

'They've murdered her and kidnapped the two children,' said Mrs. Clayton hysterically.

Mr. Clayton conducted a hasty search of the house.

'There's no trace of any of them,' he said.

At that moment came a knocking at the door, and Mrs. Clayton went down to open it.

Mrs. Fellowes stood there.

'I hope Billy got home all right,' she said.

'He's not here,' said Mrs. Clayton wildly. 'He's been kidnapped.'

'Kidnapped?'

'When did he leave your party?' said Mr. Clayton.

'Some time ago,' said Mrs. Fellowes. 'His Gryphon head got jammed and he went home. At least so the other children told me. I meant to ring you up but, what with all the uproar and little Susie Parker being sick and little Ella Poppleham cutting her head open on the fireguard and Maisie falling downstairs, I haven't had a second even to *think* till now and then I thought I might as well come round and make sure it was all right.'

'It isn't,' said Mrs. Clayton, her face stony with despair. 'They've all gone. They've been murdered and kidnapped, all of them.'

'I'm going to the police station now,' said Mr. Clayton, 'and then I'm going to scour the countryside.'

They went down to the gate and there they stopped. Two women were approaching from opposite directions. One carried a baby, the other led a small boy wearing what looked like a tattered green tunic.

'Oh, dear!' said Mrs. Clayton. 'Those two children we said we'd take in—the abandoned baby and the little acrobat. We must tell them we can't have them now. Quick, dear! I'll tell Miss Milton and you tell Mrs. Monks. There isn't a minute to spare.'

She ran down the road to Miss Milton.

'I'm so sorry, Miss Milton,' she said, 'A dreadful thing has happened. I'm afraid we can't take——' She stopped and looked down at the face of the sleeping baby. '*Peter!*' she screamed.

Mr. Clayton had approached Mrs. Monks.

'I'm very sorry, Mrs. Monks,' he said, 'but I'm afraid it will be impossible for us to——' He looked down at the small face upraised to his in a beaming smile and gave a yell of delight. '*Billy!*' he shouted.

Dusk was falling as William walked down the road. Ginger, sent on a reconnoitring expedition, had reported the course of events. One small child had seen the Outlaws entering the wood with Billy in his Gryphon suit, another had seen William and Ginger carrying the baby to the barn, and both had duly reported these facts. The net was closing round the Outlaws and they knew that retribution awaited them at home. William's steps were slow and dragging. He had put off the moment of return as long as possible, but it could be put off no longer.

Plunging his hands into his pockets with a despondent gesture he was surprised to find one of them in contact with a hard shell. The baby tortoise! He had forgotten the baby tortoise. . . . He took it out and held it on his palm. It poked its head from its shell and looked round in an inquiring fashion. The gloom cleared from his countenance.

'I'll swop you a Treacle Dab for it,' said a voice and he looked up to find Frankie Parker standing before him, gazing enviously at the tortoise.

'No,' said William.

'Two Treacle Dabs.'

'No. I won't swop it at all.'

'How did you get it?' said Frankie irritably. 'You said you hadn't any money.'

William was silent for a moment as his mind went over the events of the day, already blurred and confused by the passage of time. He straightened his drooping shoulders. Something of dignity invested his bedraggled figure.

'I got it,' he said loftily, 'by the power of thought.'

CHAPTER II

William Goes for a Nice Little Walk

'WHY are you doin' all this muddlin' about?' said William, throwing an interested glance round the disordered room.

'I'm spring cleaning, dear,' said Mrs. Brown, 'and get out of the way.'

'But it's not spring,' objected William. 'You can't do spring cleanin' when it's not spring.'

'I know it's not spring, dear, but I had 'flu in the spring and had to put it off. Now *do* get out of the way.'

'Well, I don't mind helpin' a bit with spring cleanin',' said William, his interest increasing as he inspected the chaos that surrounded him. 'I did help last year, didn't I?'

'If you call it helping,' said Mrs. Brown, plunging the vacuum cleaner attachment into the recesses of the settee. 'You scrubbed your father's chair, loose cover and all, and left it *sodden*. Dripping with water right through to the floor. He was furious. He couldn't use it for weeks.'

'Well, it was clean,' said William after a moment's thought. 'An' I'm a year older than that now. I've got a good bit more sense than I had all that time ago. An' anyway it was a *sens'ble* thing to do. That water goin' right through cleaned the inside. I bet you'd've only cleaned the outside, your way. I bet that chair's never been so clean in its life as what it was when I'd finished with it.'

'Even after it was dry it gave your father lumbago.... Do leave the vacuum alone, William.'

'I was only wonderin' how it worked. ... Well, what can I do to help?'

35

'You can go away,' said Mrs. Brown. 'You can go for a nice little walk.'

'Oh, all right,' said William distantly, 'if you don't *want* me to help . . . but I bet I *could* help all right.'

There was a look of purpose on his face as he went from the room that might have raised doubts in Mrs. Brown's mind had it not been wholly given to the curious assortment of oddments—hairpins, crumbs, pencils and even a pair of scissors—that had lodged between the arm and seat of the settee. . . . Peace seemed to descend on the house, broken only by the humming of the vacuum cleaner. He's gone for a nice little walk, thought Mrs. Brown happily, as she started on the other side of the settee. One wonders where all the dirt comes from. . . . I'll get the carpets out on to the lawn tomorrow if the weather holds. . . . The cushion covers have washed well. . . . I'll wash the curtains this afternoon. . . .

A sound from the next room cut sharply through her mellow dreams of curtain washing and carpet sweeping. She stood motionless, listening, an anxious frown on her face. Another sound came from the next room. The peace that had enveloped the house was shattered. William had not gone for a nice little walk.

Heaving a sigh, she went into the dining-room. William was scattering the last particles of a packet of tea upon the carpet.

'Well, you can't say I've not done *this* all right,' he said virtuously, as he screwed up the empty packet and threw it into the fireplace. 'I heard ole Mrs. Mexton talkin' to someone an' she said there was nothin' like the old-fashioned way of cleanin' a carpet with tea leaves. She said it was better than all these modern machines an' suchlike an'——'

'William!' gasped Mrs. Brown. 'She meant *used* tea leaves and even *they're* no use. What a frightful mess you've made!'

36

William flung out his arms in an eloquent gesture.

'Well, that's what she *said*. She said there was nothin' like the old-fashioned way of cleanin' a carpet with tea leaves. She——'

'It's going to take me *hours* to get it out.'

'But I only did same as she *said*. How was I to know she meant you'd got to make tea of 'em first? She never *said* so. She never *said* make tea of 'em first.... Tell you what!' The frown cleared from his brow. 'We could pour boilin' water on 'em on the carpet. *That*'d make 'em into used tea leaves all right.'

'No, William. You've made enough mess already.'

William repeated his eloquent gesture.

'But I keep tellin' you I only did what she *said*. She said there was nothin' like the old-fashioned way of cleanin' a carpet with tea leaves.'

Mrs. Brown raised her hand to her head.

'William, will you *stop* saying that!'

'Well, *she* said it. It wasn't me that said it. It was *her*. She said there was nothin'——'

'Will you go *out*, William!'

'Yes, but listen,' said William earnestly. 'While I was doin' those tea leaves, I thought of a new way of cleanin' the flues. You've never let me do 'em before, but I thought with it bein' spring cleanin' it'd save you time if I did it.... I mean—well, I mean I thought you'd *like* me to do it.'

'William,' said Mrs. Brown, controlling herself with difficulty, 'there's only one thing I'd like you to do and that is go out for a nice little walk.'

'All right,' said William despondently. 'But I bet you'll be sorry you didn't let me help with those flues. I bet you'll never think of the new way I've thought of. An' she just said *tea* leaves. She didn't say make tea of 'em first. She——'

'*William!*'

'All right. I'm goin'.' He assumed an air of pathos. 'Turning your own son out like a dog! An' I don't b'lieve there's any *use* in spring cleaning anyway. I b'lieve——'

He found himself addressing the empty air. Mrs. Brown had returned to the comparative peace of her spring-cleaning chaos.

He wandered down the road dejectedly, hands in pockets, head sunk between his shoulders.

'She jus' said *tea* leaves,' he muttered. 'How was I to know she meant make tea of 'em first? ... An' I *bet* I'd have cleaned those flues all right. Some people don't seem to *want* people to help 'em. It's enough to make people stop helpin' people all the rest of people's lives.'

But it was not in William's nature to remain downcast for long. Gradually his head emerged from his shoulders, his walk assumed its usual elasticity and he began to take an interest in his surroundings. There was a suspicious movement in the ditch that might have been made by a water rat, two sparrows were carrying on a spirited fight in the hedge, a horse in a field on the other side of the hedge kicked up its heels suddenly and began to gallop across the field, and a man carrying a basket came suddenly round the bend in the road. William's interest, divided till now between water rat, sparrow and horse, concentrated itself on the man who was walking with a long, springing stride down the road. He was tall, thin, dark-skinned and bearded and he wore a turban.

Without a moment's hesitation William turned in his tracks and began to walk beside him, looking up at him with unconcealed curiosity. He had never yet walked down the road with a man wearing a turban and he wanted to enjoy the experience. The man returned his scrutiny. William's hasty inspection of the flues before he laid his plans for their cleaning had left its traces across his forehead and down one cheek.

'Your face is dirty,' said the man.

He had a high-pitched staccato voice and he hunched up his shoulders as he spoke.

'I've been spring cleaning,' said William with dignity.

'Ha!' said the man. 'It is fantastic, the spring cleaning. Only the mind of a woman could have devised so tortuous a way of wasting time, energy and money.'

'Yes, that's jolly good,' said William, impressed. 'I was tryin' to say that to my mother, but I couldn't think of as good words as yours an' anyway she wasn't listenin'. I'll try'n' remember what you said. It was jolly good.'

The man set the basket down in the road, brought a pipe and tobacco pouch from his pocket, scraped the last grain of tobacco from the pouch into the pipe and proceeded to light it. William transferred his attention to the basket. A small squeak came from it.

'Is there a cat in there?' he said.

The man shook his head.

'Mice?'

Again the man shook his head.

'Guinea pig? I once had a guinea pig that made a noise like that. . . . Well, a bit like that.'

The man stooped down and opened the basket. A black face with large, soft eyes looked up at him from a nest of woolly material.

'Gosh!' gasped William. 'A monkey!'

'A langur,' said the man. 'He feels the cold. I keep shawl round him.'

'*Gosh!*' gasped William again.

The man had closed the basket and was walking on down the road. William accompanied him, his eyes glued to the basket.

'Where are you takin' it?' he said.

'To a gentleman's private zoo. He has wanted a langur for long. I bring him.'

'What's its name?'

'Tito.'

'Can I carry the basket?'

'No.'

'Can I have another look at him?'

'No,' said the man, adding with frigid courtesy: 'There is no need for me to take you farther out of your way.'

'You're not doin',' William reassured him. 'I'm goin' the way you're goin'.'

'But I am going to the station.'

'Well, that's where I'm goin',' said William promptly. 'It's a funny thing but that's where I'm goin'. I'm goin' a little walk 'cause of this spring cleanin' an' it's jus' a nice little walk to the station. I bet I'd have felt like goin' a little walk to the station, anyway. . . . What does it eat?'

'It eats specially prepared food,' said the man shortly. He had evidently had enough of William's company.

'I'll buy it from you if you'd like to sell it,' offered William. 'It'd save you the trouble of takin' it to this zoo. I've got nearly two shillin's left over from a tip an aunt gave me, so I bet I could buy it all right, an' I could look after it all right, too. I've looked after animals all my life. I've looked after dogs an' rabbits an' a guinea pig an'—an' caterpillars an'—an' I once had a c'lection of insects that was *famous*. Well, everyone round here knew about them. They nearly filled a box till most of 'em got out. A monkey'd be nothin' to me.'

'A langur,' said the man.

'I bet it'd learn to eat cabbage leaves an' lettuce leaves,' said William. 'I'd prepare 'em special, same as you said. Or dog biscuits. I've got a packet of ants' eggs, too, left over from a goldfish.'

The man surveyed the landscape in an absent fashion and made no comment.

'It might *like* ants' eggs,' went on William. 'They might be its nat'ral food. There mus' be ants in the jungle.'

The man made no comment.

'I once fed a guinea pig on ants' eggs,' continued

William. 'It died but I don't think it died of ants' eggs. I think it died of some other disease.'

They reached the station. The man walked on to the platform. After a moment's hesitation William followed him. A train drew in. The man entered a carriage. After a moment's hesitation William followed him.

'I'll jus' stay till it's time for the train to go,' he said. He put his ear to the basket, 'I can hear it breathin'. Let's have another look at it, shall we? Jus' to make sure it's all right.'

The man had taken out his tobacco pouch and an expression of consternation flashed into his thin brown face.

'My tobacco! I meant to buy more tobacco. There was a shop just outside the station. Your presence distracted me.' He looked from William to the basket in a harrassed, speculative fashion. 'Keep your eye on him just for a moment till I return. I will run quickly to the shop and back. I will be here again before the train goes.'

William watched the man run lightly down the platform and vanish through the exit. Almost immediately the guard waved his flag and the train began to steam slowly out of the station. William leaned out of the window. . . . The turbaned figure was running wildly along the platform in its wake, waving its arms and shouting unintelligibly in a high-pitched voice. The train gathered speed. The shouting figure became a mere dot in the distance. The train turned a corner and the dot disappeared. . . . William drew a deep breath and sat beside his charge. Cautiously he opened the basket and the little face looked up at him again with soft, dark eyes and made friendly chattering sounds.

A thrill of pride and excitement swept over William as he closed the basket. He began to embellish the adventure in his mind in order to relate it more impressively to his friends. . . . 'Well, this man, he said he'd got to do some shoppin' an' would I take this valu'ble monkey along for him to the train. He wouldn't have trusted anyone else with

41

this valu'ble monkey, but soon as he saw me he knew I was the sort of boy that could be trusted with a valu'ble monkey....'

The train drew up at a station and it occurred to William for the first time to wonder whither he and his charge were bound. He looked at the label on the basket ... Steedham. The next station but one.

Assuming the responsible air of a boy entrusted with a valuable monkey, he sat close to the basket, keeping one hand on it and occasionally leaning down to apply his ear to it and murmur encouraging words to the occupant.

'Good ole Tito.... Good ole boy.... How're you gettin' on, ole boy?... Cheer up, ole Tito....'

The langur made small noises in reply which William interpreted as expressions of friendliness and interest. The train wound slowly through the countryside and pulled up sleepily at Steedham station.

William took the basket and descended on to the platform.

Asked for his ticket, he gave a comparatively accurate account of what had happened. The porter scratched his head. It was a situation that had never before arisen in the whole course of his career, and he didn't know how to deal with it.

'You'll have to wait 'til the nex' train come in,' he said at last, 'and that's not till another hour.'

'All right,' said William.

He sat on the seat with his basket beside him for what seemed an interminable length of time. Then he got up and approached the porter.

'That train mus' be jolly late,' he said. 'It's more than an hour since I got here.'

'It's five minutes exact,' said the porter shortly.

It was at this point that an irresistible temptation swept over William. He wanted to walk down the road like the turbaned man, carelessly carrying a monkey in a basket.

He'd be back at the station long before the train came in. He picked up the basket.

'Jus' goin' for a little walk,' he said airily to the porter.

The porter stood scratching his head in a fresh access of perplexity as William made his way through the barrier and out into the road.

There he walked with an elaborately long, springing stride. He was tall and thin and dark-skinned and turbaned. He carried a monkey in a basket—a monkey that he had saved from the attack of a savage leopard in darkest Africa. Or perhaps darkest India. No. . . . He reconstructed the story. He had taken a thorn from the monkey's foot in the jungle and later, when he was captured by cannibals and was just going to be eaten alive, the monkey had leapt down from a tree and gnawed through his bonds and ever since had been his inseparable companion. No. . . . He thought of a better one still. He had rescued the monkey from a circus where he was being ill-treated, and already a gang of circus men—ruthless, cruel desperadoes—were on his track. He quickened his pace and glanced back warily over his shoulder. The circus men were not in sight . . . but perhaps they had taken a short cut across the countryside and were waiting for him at the next bend in the road. They would be heavily armed, of course. They would stick at nothing. They would probably kidnap both him and the monkey.

He stopped. He was passing a large gateway decorated with flags. Through the gateway he could see an extensive stretch of park-like grounds and behind the trees, the outline of a stately mansion.

A large notice announced 'Steedham Garden Fête', and a trickle of people was going through the gate. William watched with interest. In the distance he could see a roundabout and a hoop-la stall. William always found roundabouts and hoop-la stalls irresistible. An idea occurred to him. He could throw off the gang of circus men

43

(though already they were fading in the light of reality), enjoy a ride on the roundabout and a few throws at the hoop-la stall, and be back at the station before the turbaned man's train arrived.

He entered the grounds and wandered down a broad path towards the lawn from which came the heartening strains of the roundabout. Then he considered his basket. ... You couldn't go on a roundabout with a basket. He looked about him. There was a row of stalls under the trees by the edge of the lawn. One, piled high with an accumulation of junk, had a notice, 'Bring and Buy Stall'. It appeared to have neither customers nor stall holder. William approached it. Beneath it were several baskets not unlike the one he was carrying. He would leave his basket among them (no one would notice it), have his roundabout ride, then retrieve it and be waiting on the platform by the time the train came in. He wedged the basket as unobtrusively as possible between two others and set off at a run towards the roundabout.

Turning a bend in the path, he collided with a tall, elderly, monocled man who stood talking to a clergyman.

'Look where you're going, my boy,' said the monocled man.

'Sorry,' said William breathlessly as he plunged on to his goal.

'No manners, the young of today,' said the monocled man severely as he watched William's fleeing figure. 'No manners, no consideration, no courtesy, no chivalry, no respect for law and order.'

'Exactly, Sir Gervase,' said the clergyman. 'Different from our generation, indeed. I always think how kind of you it is to throw your grounds open to the public on this occasion.'

'A pleasure,' said Sir Gervase. 'A pleasure, I assure you.'

'You haven't included the private zoo this year. Perhaps as well.'

'Yes. . . . Some of the animals are a little nervous and the children are apt to feed them on unsuitable diet. . . . I'm expecting a fresh inmate this afternoon, by the way. A friend has sent me a langur from India and his agent is delivering it to me this afternoon. But I'm rather worried about my zoo.'

'Oh, dear! Why?'

'Well, it turns out there's an old right of way running through it. My father and the man who owned the adjoining property were old cronies—both keen fishermen—and my father gave him a right of way through these grounds. It's not been used for years, but now a nephew of this other chap has inherited the property and he's going to run up a building estate in Five Acre Meadow and he's claiming the right of way for his wretched lorries. Clean through my zoo. It'll ruin the place. . . . I'm sure I once heard my father say that the right of way had been relinquished, but I can't find any proof of it. The solicitors have no record. . . . Well, there the thing is and apparently I can't get round it. I'll even have to knock the walls down.'

'Distressing,' said the clergyman.

'I use a stronger word,' said Sir Gervase with an eagle flash of his blue eyes. 'A word hardly fit for your ears, my dear Vicar. Ah, here, I think, is the man who was bringing my langur but——'

The tall, thin, turbaned man was making his way through the crowd, his face wearing an expression of acute anguish.

'Sir Gervase, is it not?' he panted as he reached the two.

'Yes,' said Sir Gervase. 'Where's the langur?'

'It has been stolen,' said the man dramatically. 'Stolen from under my very eyes.'

'Good Lord!' said Sir Gervase. 'Who stole it?'

'A boy,' said the man. 'Young in years but dyed deep in crime. A boy with a dirty face.'

'A boy——' Sir Gervase and the clergyman looked at

each other. 'Good Heavens! That boy who charged into us just now!'

'Dirt across his forehead and down a cheek.'

'That's the one!' said Sir Gervase. 'Come on! Let's look for the young scoundrel and you can tell us what happened as we go.'

A hasty search revealed no sign of the young scoundrel. 'I expect he is far away by now,' said the turbaned man with a shrug of his thin shoulders.

But William was not far away. In fact he was quite near, burrowing frantically beneath the Bring and Buy stall for his basket. It wasn't there. It had vanished. There seemed to be baskets of every shape and size, containing every conceivable article from roller skates to Bath buns, but *his* basket with its precious occupant had vanished. His grimy face tense with horror, he rummaged on the stall itself, turning over household stores, tea cosies, Victorian ornaments and woolly toys ... till a woman in a pink jumper and fur stole accosted him indignantly.

'How *dare* you disarrange all our things like that?' she said. 'What on earth do you think you're doing?'

'Looking for a monkey,' said William desperately.

'Don't be impertinent,' said the woman. 'And go away. Go *away*!'

The ferocity of her tone startled William so much that the flat iron he was holding slipped from his grasp on to a punnet of new-laid eggs and, aghast at this fresh damage, he fled down a tree-bordered path, stopping when he found he was not being pursued and looking up at the trees in the vain hope of seeing the monkey there. He didn't see the monkey, but, seated on the grass under a beech tree, with a basket between them, were two middle-aged women. They were obviously sisters, dressed alike in neat grey suits, except that one wore a brown beret and the other a blue beret.

But it was not on the women that William's widening

eyes fastened themselves. It was on the basket. There was something familiar about the basket. So many baskets had he investigated as he burrowed beneath the Bring and Buy stall that his impressions had become a little blurred, but there was certainly something familiar about the basket. He approached the couple tentatively.

'I don't think that people have brought and bought as well as they did last year,' Blue Beret was saying, 'but it's always an interesting stall to help at . . . and now for lunch. An excellent idea of yours to bring a picnic lunch, dear.'

'Yes,' said Brown Beret with a little secret smile, 'and I've prepared a very *special* lunch. I'm not going to let you know what it is till I've opened the basket. It's a surprise.'

'I don't somehow remember the basket,' said Blue Beret, looking at it reflectively.

'Oh, yes, dear,' said Brown Beret carelessly. 'They're all alike, these baskets. We've got several in the box room, you know. I went up and chose a largish one because of the special lunch I was making and——'

'Please——' panted William urgently.

'Go away, boy,' said Blue and Brown Beret simultaneously.

'Look at his *face*,' said Blue Beret dispassionately.

'Have you no manners, boy?' said Brown Beret. 'Go away. . . . And now, dear, I'm going to open the basket and make your mouth water.'

Slowly she began to raise the lid.

'You'll adore every morsel of it. You'll——'

She gave a shrill scream as Tito sprang out of the basket, seized the brown beret from her head, and, his long tail swinging, shot up the beech tree and ran fleetly along an overhanging branch.

Shouts rose up from all sides. There was an excited rush of people to the foot of the beech tree.

'The langur!' shouted Sir Gervase.

'Tito!' screamed the turbaned man.

'Is this your idea of a joke, dear?' said Blue Beret plaintively.

Buzzing with excitement, the crowd surged along the path as Tito, pausing a moment to put the brown beret on his head, swung himself from branch to branch. Then a gasp went up. Tito had reached a branch that stretched to the mansion itself and, swinging to the end of it, leapt nimbly in through an open window and vanished from view.

Beyond control, the crowd surged in at the front door.

'He's come downstairs.'

'He's in the library.'

'He's on top of the bookcase.'

'I still don't understand it, dear. Did you *know* there was a monkey in the basket?'

The crowd poured into the library. There on top of the bookcase was Tito, prancing exultantly, chattering at the crowd. Then he began to take the leather-bound books from the top shelf and hurl them down upon the heads below. Receiving the impact of hard leather bindings, the heads began to withdraw. Only Sir Gervase held his ground, picking up the books one by one as they showered down on him. Several of the bindings came adrift from their moorings and he retrieved them tenderly.

'A unique collection,' he said, 'and the little devil's ruining it. Can't say I've ever read any of them myself, but there they've been ever since I can remember. My father thought the world of them.' He bent down to pick up a large tome with a rubbed morocco binding. 'Horace.... My father was great on Horace. Read him in season and out of season. In the original, of course. He—Good Heavens! What's this?'

A folded paper had dropped from between the pages. He picked it up and examined it. Even his monocle seemed to dance with excitement.

'Good *Lord*! It's some sort of legal document.... Yes.

48

Tito hurled the valuable books to the floor

Listen. The old chap relinquishes his right of way in return for the fishing rights in that part of the river that runs at the bottom of the grounds. Legal, all right. Signed, sealed and witnessed. Drawn up in the North of Scotland. I suppose the old chaps were having a fishing holiday there so no wonder the solicitor couldn't trace it. Well,' he turned to the turbaned man, 'this is a good day's work.'

But the man in the turban wasn't interested. He was making small caressing noises to the langur. At last the langur, as if noticing him for the first time, jumped suddenly down from the bookcase and flung itself into his arms, nestling affectionately against his shoulder.

Sir Gervase patted its head.

'So the little chap can have a nice quiet home in the zoo, after all. No highways, no lorries. Ha, ha!'

'My Tito,' murmured the turbaned man. 'What you must have suffered at the hands of that villain!'

Then he turned and saw William standing in the forefront of the group of spectators. His hand shot out accusingly.

'The thief! The boy! The boy with the dirty face!'

Sir Gervase adjusted his monocle, which had come adrift during the proceedings, and inspected William with interest.

'Ah, yes. . . . The boy with the dirty face. We have met before, I believe. And are you, my boy, responsible for all this?'

'W-well, in a sort of a way,' said William hoarsely, looking round for escape. 'I mean, I can 'splain all about it . . . I mean, you see, it was like this——'

Sir Gervase raised his hand.

'Explanations are tedious,' he said. 'Let us leave it at that. Your activities have caused a certain amount of confusion. I am no deep student of character, but I should imagine that your activities usually do. However, I have to thank you for the discovery of a valuable legal document so

50

we will draw a veil over the rest of the proceedings.'

'Me draw no veil,' said the turbaned man indignantly. 'He steal my Tito. He let him loose among the trees. He risk his precious life. He——'

He stopped. William had tactfully withdrawn and was forcing a way out through the crowd. At the door Blue Beret was still harping on her grievances.

'I said from the beginning that it looked a different sort of basket—I *knew* it was a different sort of basket—but you wouldn't listen.' Her eye fell on William and lit up with gloomy interest. 'The boy! The boy who was hanging around! I believe he knows something about it. I believe——'

But William was already making good his retreat down the drive.

He found his way to the station, bought a ticket with an air of assurance that left the porter speechless, saw the train just moving out of the platform, flung himself into a passing carriage, picked himself up, leant out of the window, gave a dignified salute to the gaping porter and settled down for the journey.

As his mind went over the events of the afternoon, the memory that stood out most clearly was the memory of Tito prancing on the top of the bookcase and hurling books down on to the crowd below, and he was conscious of a deep almost irresistible longing to hurl books himself from the top of a bookcase on to a crowd below. He felt that life could never be quite complete till he had done it.

Reaching home, he sauntered into the sitting-room, where Mrs. Brown was sewing a cushion into a cushion cover.

'They've washed much better than I thought they would,' she said complacently, 'Well, dear, did you have a nice little walk?'

'Yes, thank you,' said William. 'I took a valu'ble monkey in a basket to Steedham an' it got loose an' found a valu'ble legal document, so they didn't mind.'

'What nonsense you talk, dear!' said Mrs. Brown placidly, as she fastened off a thread and plumped the cushion into shape. 'Yes, it looks almost as good as new. . . . I really think I shall have finished the spring cleaning by the end of the week.'

William hunched his shoulders and spoke in a high-pitched staccato voice.

'Only a woman could——' He hunted in his memory for the words the man in the turban had used, finally giving up the attempt and ending lamely, 'Well, anyway only a woman could have.'

'I've been thinking, dear,' said Mrs. Brown.

She paused. During William's absence she had felt pangs of remorse. She had rejected William's well-meant offers of help. She was always rejecting William's well-meant offers of help. And always afterwards she felt pangs of remorse. . . . Even over the tea leaves he had meant well. She ought to have found some little job for him to do that he couldn't go wrong over. And while he was out on his little walk she thought she had found one.

'Yes?' said William.

'Well, dear, if you *really* want to help with the spring cleaning, you might dust the books in the dining-room book shelves. It's a nice quiet little job and will be a great help to me.'

A gleam came into William's eye. He would fetch Ginger and they would re-enact the scene. First he would be the monkey on the bookcase and Ginger the crowd below. Then Ginger could be the monkey on the bookcase and he'd be the crowd below. . . . The crowd might retaliate and throw the books back. Yes, that would make the whole thing more exciting. It would make it into a sort of a duel. He and Ginger were experts in duels. They had had duels with potatoes, rotten apples, lumps of coal and even begonia tubers ... but they had never tried books before.... He'd dust them properly, of course, he assured himself, sternly quelling the small stirrings of his conscience. He'd be helping with the spring cleaning, all right. He'd put them all back in their places afterwards. Well, it would do them *good* to get thrown about a bit. It would take the dust off the inside of the pages. And they might find a valuable legal document....

'May I go and get Ginger to help?' he said.

'If you like, dear,' said Mrs. Brown doubtfully. Misgivings had suddenly assailed her. 'But surely you can do it alone?'

'No, you can't,' said William. 'You've got to have two.'

'Well, you'll do it thoroughly, won't you?' said Mrs. Brown. 'You'll take them all out?'

'Yes, we'll take 'em all out,' promised William.

'And wash your face and make a nice quiet job of it. The book dusting, I mean.' Her misgivings were increasing. 'Just take them out quietly one by one and——'

But William was already out of earshot, hastening down the road to summon his fellow campaigner to the fray.

CHAPTER III

William the Tree-Dweller

'WELL, we've not fixed up how to get to the moon yet,' said William.

'We've tried lots of ways,' Ginger reminded him.

The two, having been turned out of Ginger's house by Ginger's mother because she wanted to make a cake without fear of constant raids on the ingredients, were making their way slowly along the road to William's house.

'Yes, but none of them have come off,' said William. 'We've got to keep on tryin' till somethin' does come off. Somethin's sure to come off sooner or later. Stands to reason it will. That's what happened to all the inventors in hist'ry. They went on tryin' an' tryin' an' in the end it came off.'

'Yes, but you don't know about all the ones that tried an' tried an' tried an' it didn't come off.'

'That's right!' Keep on makin' objections!' said William irritably. 'Here I am tryin' to help civ'lisation an' the yuman race by gettin' them to the moon an' all you can do is to keep on makin' objections.'

'Well, you've got to have a rocket to get to the moon,' said Ginger, 'an' we've not got one.'

'I don't think a rocket's all that necess'ry,' said William after a moment's consideration. 'They've kept tryin' with it an' they've not done it yet. I shouldn't be surprised if this fuel they're usin' isn't too strong. It prob'ly goes too far. It prob'ly goes *miles* farther than the moon an' that's no good. They'll end by smashin' up the moon altogether an' then no one can get to it.'

'Well, what ought they to use?' said Ginger.

'I've been thinkin' ... I think they ought to start with somethin' quite small an' sort of work their way up gradual to big things.... You know, I can shoot a t'riffic distance with that new bow an' arrow of mine.'

'Well, you couldn't get to the moon with a bow an' arrow.'

'I never said you could,' said William. 'You jus' don't wait to see what I'm goin' to say. You start makin' objections the moment I open my mouth. You'd never get anythin' done for civ'lisation an' the yuman race if everyone started makin' objections the minute anyone else opened their mouth. Well'—with heavy sarcasm—'it's news to *me* if you'd get anythin' done for civ'lisation an'

54

the yuman race if everyone started makin' objections the minute anyone else opened their mouth.'

'Oh, all right,' said Ginger. 'Go on.'

'Well,' said William, 'I shouldn't be surprised if that las' shot of mine didn't get half way to the moon—well, quarter, anyway—an' what I thought was if we had somethin' that'd sort of give it an extra shoot—I mean somethin' on *top* of its ordin'ry shoot. . . .'

'What?' said Ginger, adding in a slightly belligerent tone, 'Well, you can't say I'm makin' objections when I jus' say "what?", can you?'

'No, that's all right,' said William kindly. 'I don't mind ordinary questions. . . . Well, what I thought was that if we could get a specially strong firework an' fix it to the end of this new arrow of mine an' let it off—the firework, I mean —jus' when I'm shootin' off the arrow, it'd go up jolly high an' then when we'd got into the way of it we'd put another firework on an' then another an' then another an' so on till we'd got it strong enough to get there.'

'Ummmm,' said Ginger dubiously. 'Where do we get the fireworks?' adding, 'Well, *that's* an ordin'ry question, isn't it?'

'Oh, yes, that's all right,' said William. 'Well, it's the Fifth of November nex' week so there ought to be lots of fireworks about. My father gen'rally gives me a box of fireworks but he doesn't gen'rally give it to me till the axshull day an' we want to start this shootin' business straight off.'

'Ask him to let you have jus' one today. He might be in a good temper.'

'He's not in a good temper,' said William. 'He's in a bad temper 'cause of Mr. Redditch.'

Mr. Redditch had recently come to live near the Browns. He was a boastful, self-important little man to whom Mr. Brown had taken an immediate and not unjustifiable dislike. Mr. Redditch had joined the golf club of which Mr. Brown was a member and had first earned his dislike by taking advantage of a convenient stroke to appropriate to his use a treasured new ball of Mr. Brown's, leaving to Mr. Brown a weary veteran of his own ... and he continued to earn it by holding up the entire course while he knelt down to his putts and generally took his ease on the fairway.

Moreover, he went to London by the same train and generally in the same compartment as Mr. Brown and dispelled his morning peace by incessant prattle. He talked of himself—his cleverness, his popularity, his outstanding ability in every field of life. He told rambling pointless stories, all redounding in one way or another to his own credit. No longer could Mr. Brown read his morning paper from end to end during his morning journey up to town. Exasperation prevented his reading even two consecutive sentences.

And Mr. Redditch's enormities did not end there. He insisted on having the window shut, whatever the weather; he pushed his way into the railway carriage in front of Mr. Brown in order to secure Mr. Brown's favourite corner seat; having watched Mr. Brown playing bridge at the golf club one wet afternoon, he spent the next morning's journey telling him of his mistakes. Mr. Brown's irritation was gathering strength and his family began to look forward with trepidation to his evening return from work. Furthermore, Mr. Redditch had taken to borrowing garden implements, seizing the opportunity when Mr. Brown was out of the house and Mrs. Brown's pliant amiability made her an easy prey.

'What's Mr. Redditch got to do with it?' said Ginger.

'He makes him mad,' said William simply. 'Gosh! He was mad when he came home yesterday an' found he'd borrowed the saw.'

'You could try him,' said Ginger.

'Yes, I'll try him,' said William. 'I bet he wouldn't give me one jus' to mess about with, but if I explain that we're doin' 'speriments for civ'lisation an' the yuman race——'

'Yes, circumstances alter cases,' said Ginger, adding self-consciously, 'I read that in a book. It means the same as what you said but it's better English.'

'There's nothin' wrong with my English,' said William with spirit. 'I can talk it, can't I, an' no one can do more with it than that. That's what it's *for*, isn't it?'

'All right,' said Ginger. They had reached the gate of the Browns' homestead. 'Well, go in an' ask him.'

'All right. I'll go in an' ask him,' said William, something of his self-confidence oozing away from him as he spoke.

'Well, go on.'

'All right,' said William testily. 'Give me time to *breathe*.'

He walked up to the front door with a gait that held a mixture of swagger and reluctance—the reluctance predominating as he neared the door. He hesitated for a few moments, then vanished inside ... to return almost immediately afterwards, looking heated and outraged.

'Wouldn't even listen to me,' he said. 'Jus' shouted "No!" at me. Wouldn't even let me explain. Jus' shouted "No!" at me again. He was still mad about that saw an' because this Mr. Redditch had been tellin' him what was wrong with his golf. Gosh! Fancy anyone tellin' him there was anythin' wrong with his golf! Why, he's won *spoons* for golf. . . . Anyway, my mother said I'd better get out, so I did. He'd have started bein' vi'lent in another minute.'

'Well, what are we goin' to do now?' said Ginger.

'An' me only tryin' to help sci'nce an' civ'lisation an' the yuman race!' said William, throwing his arms out in an eloquent gesture. 'Jus' gettin' shouted "No!" at when all I'm tryin' to do is to help sci'nce an' civ'lisation an' the yuman race!'

'I s'pose he jus' thought you wanted a firework,' said Ginger mildly.

'I tried to tell him, but he wouldn't listen.'

'Well, come on. Let's try mine.'

Though Ginger's father proved as unaccommodating as Mr. Brown, an uncle of Ginger's, who had just returned from a city luncheon and was taking a more mellowed view of life, produced the sum of five shillings and sixpence which, in its turn, produced a formidable-looking rocket in a brightly-coloured wrapper.

They made their way back to William's garden. There, when William had fetched his bow and arrow from his bedroom and a box of matches from the top of the kitchen stove, they selected the middle of the lawn as the scene of the great experiment.

'That'll give us enough room jus' to start with,' said William. 'When we get to usin' six or seven of them we'll need a bigger place of course. P'raps if it's a success the government'll give us an airfield for it. . . . Now we'll fix the rocket to the end of the arrow an' you light the rocket the same time I shoot off the arrow. . . . Gosh! I shouldn't be s'prised if it makes a supersonic bang.'

They fixed the rocket on to the end of the arrow and William stretched the bow to its utmost length.

'Now you light a match,' he said 'an' put it to the rocket an' the minute it catches I'll let off the arrow. Now wait . . . One . . . Two . . . Three . . . *Go!*'

They had not seen William's father coming down the garden path, his brow wreathed in thunder clouds of wrath, carrying in his hand what was left of the saw recently borrowed by Mr Redditch. He had only just discovered it, propped up inside the garden gate, returned without ceremony or acknowledgement or thanks, the edges flattened, the blade bent and distorted. It was evident that as a sawer of logs Mr. Redditch belonged to the amateur class. Mr. Brown was fuming with inward rage as he carried his maimed treasure towards the tool shed. He was composing the highly-coloured speech that he would deliver to Mr. Redditch at their next meeting. The fact that Mr. Redditch

The rocket sped straight to a soft and yielding target

had gone away for a week's holiday and that he could not immediately give vent to his eloquence added fuel to the fire of his wrath.

Culling his choicest flowers of rhetoric and invective, he did not notice the two boys on the lawn till William's strident '*Go!*' cut sharply through the air. Then he turned ... to receive a smouldering, spluttering rocket full in the stomach with such force that he sat down heavily on the ground, while the saw performed a semicircle in the air and came to rest in the middle of a rose bush.

He flung the rocket aside and rose slowly and ponderously to his feet. His face was a beetroot hue and he was breathing heavily. It was clear that emotion had temporarily deprived him of the power of speech but it was equally clear that when the power of speech returned it would be both pointed and pungent. William hastened to make the most of the short time at his disposal.

'We didn't mean to do that,' he said. 'I'm sorry. We didn't *mean* to do it ... Listen ... We fixed the rocket on to the end of the arrow an' we meant it to go *with* the arrow. We didn't know it would come loose an' go straight for you like what it did. We didn't *know* it would. We didn't *mean* it to. We——'

Mr. Brown had recovered the power of speech but was tempering it with iron self-control.

'Give me that bow and arrow,' he said.

William handed him the bow and Ginger retrieved the arrow from a potted hydrangea and brought it to him.

'I shall destroy this,' said Mr. Brown grimly, 'and I shall never allow you to have a bow and arrow again. Do you understand?'

'But——'

'Be quiet! Have you any more of those—those fireworks?'

'No, but——'

'And you shan't have any. You're to have no more fireworks. Please understand that. If you have any given you I shall confiscate them.'

'But, Dad, it's Guy Fawkes day nex' week.'

'I'm quite aware of that,' said Mr. Brown, bending down to rub his ankle, which had got slightly twisted in his fall, 'and you're to have no fireworks for it. Nor are you to attend any firework display.'

'But, Dad,' pleaded William, 'it—it's a sort of *juty* to have fireworks on Guy Fawkes day. This Guy Fawkes man, he—he——' William had always been a little vague as to the exact role played by Guy Fawkes in history. 'He tried to save the country from havin' a Parliament. We ought to celebrate him same as we do Nelson an' St. George an'—an' Dick Turpin an' all the others. It's our *juty* to.' He searched wildly for some reason that would appeal to his father. 'I bet people'll think I'm a communist if I don't have fireworks on Guy Fawkes day. I bet I'll get put in prison for a communist an'——'

'Be *quiet*!' said Mr. Brown. He drew a deep breath and continued, 'Haven't you any sense at all? Are you a complete and utter imbecile? Haven't you any ideas in your head but tomfoolery and wanton destruction? You aren't fit to be a member of a civilised community and you seem to grow less fit with every day that passes. If you choose to go playing the fool, damaging property and endangering the life and limb of everyone around you, you must take the consequences.'

'Yes, but listen, Dad,' said William. 'I wasn't playin' the fool. I was doin' a sci'ntific experiment for civ'lisation an' the yuman race. If I'd jus' been playin' the fool, I wouldn't mind takin' what you said, but with it bein' a sci'ntific experiment makes it diff'rent.'

'Circumstances alter cases,' murmured Ginger, coming to the help of his friend as best he could.

'Be *quiet*!' roared Mr. Brown, 'and be off, both of you!'

'But, Dad,' began William, standing his ground till Mr.

Brown advanced on him, the light of purpose in his eye, then beating a hasty retreat, scrambling through the hedge with Ginger at his heels.

'Gosh!' he panted when he reached the safety of the road. 'He jus' wouldn't listen an'—Gosh! No fireworks on Guy Fawkes day!'

'We ought to've tied it tighter,' said Ginger.

But William was less interested in his experiment than in his grievances.

'Jus' sat down ordin'ry an' didn't hurt himself at all. . . . Why, there's people that have given their *lives* for sci'ntific experiments—atom bombs an' radium an' suchlike—without makin' as much fuss as he made jus' sittin' down ordin'ry. Some people'd be *int'rested* in sci'ntific experiments an' gettin' to the moon, but he didn't seem to be. No,'—with his short, sarcastic laugh—'I mus' say *he* didn't seem to be int'rested in them. Jus' went on at me as if I was a crim'nal. There's some people that'd be proud to have people in their fam'lies that did sci'ntific experiments for civ'lisation an' the yuman race. Gosh! It isn't a *crime* to try'n' help civ'lisation an' the yuman race. Well, it's news to *me* if it is. It's news to *me* if it's a crime to try'n' help civ'lisation an' the yuman race. It——'

'Well, how are we goin' to manage without fireworks?' said Ginger, hastening to stem the tide of William's eloquence before it reached flood proportions. 'I bet my uncle won't give me any more.'

'Gosh! Didn't he carry on!' said William, who was never easily diverted from his theme. 'Sayin' I wasn't fit to be a member of a civ'lised community! Well, I jolly well don't *want* to be a member of one. I'm jolly well *sick* of civ'lised communities. I'm jolly well *sick* of tryin' to help civ'lisation an' the yuman race. All I get for it is my bow an' arrow took off me an' no fireworks. That *shows* civ'lisation's all wrong an' I'm jus' about fed up with it. I'm jolly well goin' back to the days before there *was* any civ'lisation. I bet everyone was a jolly sight better off before it started. I bet we'd all be a jolly sight better off if we all went back to bein' savages same as those ole Markie was tellin' us about that lived in trees.'

'Tree-dwellers,' said Ginger.

'Yes, them. . . . Well, I'm jolly well goin' back to bein' one. I'd sooner live in a tree than a house any day. Gosh!' —his gloom lightened as he warmed to his new theme— 'an' we could, too! There's lots of trees round here. We could start bein' tree-dwellers straight away an' I bet it'd sort of set the fashion an' everyone'd start doin' it an' it'd be the end of civ'lisation an' a jolly good thing, too!'

'I dunno that *everyone*'d want to live in trees,' said Ginger thoughtfully.

'I don't see why not,' said William. 'They're always grumblin' what a lot their houses cost them. Rates an' things. An' trees are *free*, aren't they? Well, it's news to *me* if trees aren't free.'

'The rain'd come in.'

'You could fix somethin' up to keep the rain off. An' they're jolly comfortable, are trees, 'cause I've tried 'em. They wouldn't need furniture if they got the right sort of tree. There's branches that make jolly good tables an' chairs. You could have meals in 'em. I've et lots of things in trees an' they tasted a jolly sight nicer than the things you eat in houses. I——' He stopped suddenly. They were passing a house in the garden of which grew a tree with broad, spreading branches. 'That looks a good one. I'd like to try that one.'

'Gosh, you can't, William. Someone lives there.'

'Well, I keep tellin' you trees are free. Come to that, the whole earth's free for savages, so now we've started bein' savages the whole earth's free to us.'

Ginger considered this argument with frowning brows. It seemed unanswerable.

'Well, I dunno . . .' he said at last.

'There's no one about, anyway,' said William. 'An' no one'll see us once we're in it. We can use it for practice an' then when we've found out how it works we can go an' find an impenetrable forest to tree-dwell in.'

'Yes, but——' began Ginger and stopped.

William had already crossed the lawn and, after an agile leap, was dangling by his hands from the lowest branch. Ginger hesitated a moment then followed him.

'It's a jolly easy tree,' came William's voice from beyond the first two branches. 'It's jus' like a ladder. You go up an' up as easy as easy. Come on.'

Ginger swung his solid form on to the lowest branch and began to scramble from branch to branch. He found William comfortably ensconced on a branch near the top.

'This is a jolly good branch,' said William. 'I think I could sleep on this one. Look! I can stretch my legs out on it an' lean against the trunk. An' you could have the one opposite. It's nearly the same shape. An' the one underneath would make a good table. We could put things on it an'——'

The door of the house opened and a voice called:

'Tinker!'

'Gosh! That's Miss Hopkins,' whispered Ginger. 'I forgot she lived here. She lives here with her sister. An' that ole Tinker's her cat.'

'Well, let's stay quite still,' said William. 'She can't see us 'cause of the leaves an' she'll soon go in.'

'Tinker! Tinker! Tinker! Tinker! Tinker! Tinker! TINKER! What *can* have happened to him?'

Another voice answered. Evidently Miss Hopkins' sister had joined her in the garden.

'Perhaps he's up the tree, dear. He does sometimes go up the tree, you know.'

'Well, if he's up the tree we won't worry about him. He can get up and down quite easily.'

'Miaow!' cried William raucously.

It was his instinctive reaction to the suggestion that if Tinker was in the tree no further investigations would be made. He realised as soon as he had uttered the sound that it was a mistake.

There was a sudden silence.

'He is in the tree,' said one voice, 'and I think I can see him. I can see *something*.'

'It didn't sound like Tinker,' said the other.

'It must have been Tinker.'

'I'm worried, dear,' said the first voice. 'I wish it had sounded more like Tinker.'

'Miaow!' said William, trying to sound more like Tinker.

'It *is* Tinker,' said the second voice, 'but he doesn't sound himself somehow.'

'No, there was a note in it almost as if he were in distress. . . . Or in pain.'

'Certainly upset about something.'

'Let's get a saucer of milk and put it at the foot of the tree. He may see it and come down.'

Their footsteps retreated to the house.

'Gosh! You've been an' done it now!' said Ginger. 'I s'pose you'll go down an' lap up the milk.'

'Oh, shut up,' said William, adding in a tone of disgust as his mind went back over various incidents in the past, 'It *would* be a cat! Cats! The muddles I've got into over cats! I've never had any luck with them.'

'Here's the milk,' said a voice from below.

'Put it right against the trunk, dear, where he can see it. Let's wait and see if he comes down.'

'What we've got to do now,' whispered William, 'is to make 'em think it's *not* a cat in the tree. Let's try'n think of somethin'.'

It was at this point that Ginger lost his head, raising his voice in a hoarse bark. 'Bow-wow-wow!'

'Oh, *listen*!' screamed Miss Hopkins. 'He's groaning.'

'It sounded more like a cough to me. He must have got another attack of bronchitis, poor darling!'

'You chump!' whispered William. 'You don't have dogs in trees. Let's be birds quick!'

A clamorous squawking rang out from the shelter of the leaves . . . and Miss Hopkins gave another little scream of dismay.

'He's getting hysterical. He must be in the most dreadful pain. Let's ring up the vet. at once.'

'We'll have to get him down first. We can hardly expect the vet. to climb the tree to examine him.'

'What about borrowing Mr. Redditch's ladder?'

'He's gone away, dear, and we don't know where it is. . . . No, I've got a better idea. I'll get the clothes-line prop and *prod* him down and you must stand ready to catch him.'

'Hold on tight!' whispered William.

'Let's try'n' do somethin' to frighten them,' said Ginger. 'I bet I could roar like a lion. I—*Ow!*'

A long, narrow pole had appeared suddenly through the branches and caught him violently in the chest. He grabbed hold of William. Both lost their balance and crashed through the branches to the ground. The Misses Hopkins stared in incredulous amazement at the sudden descent of two grubby small boys from the tree. Then the elder one pointed an accusing finger.

'So *you* are the boys who have been *torturing* our poor darling Tinker up in that tree.'

'No, we haven't,' said William indignantly as he scrambled to his feet. 'We haven't been torchering anything up in that tree. We've *been* torchered, more like. We——'

'Don't dare to deny it,' snapped Miss Hopkins. 'We heard the poor dumb creature's groans and cries for help.'

'It wasn't,' said Ginger. 'It was dogs an' birds an'——'

'Trespassing in our garden and torturing our cat!' said Miss Hopkins, her voice trembling with passion. 'We'll see what your father has to say about it.'

She came towards them, brandishing the clothes prop and, for the second time that day, William and Ginger chose discretion as the better part of valour, plunging out of the gate ... down the road ... and in at another gate that stood conveniently open.

'We'll hide in here 'case she's comin' after us,' said William, taking refuge behind a rhododendron bush.

'She's not comin' after us,' panted Ginger, 'but she was standing' at the gate an' saw us come in.'

'Oh, well, it's all right if she's not comin' after us,' said William, emerging from his hiding place and looking about him. 'Gosh! *That*'s a good tree.'

'You're not goin' to go *on* with it, are you, William?' said Ginger. 'Tree-dwellin', I mean. Not after all that!'

' 'Course I am,' said William, walking round the tree and looking up at it in a speculative fashion. 'I said I was goin' to be a tree-dweller an' I'm jolly well goin' to *be* one. I'm not goin' to be put off by a little thing like that. If I'm goin' to get into a row for trespassin' in one garden, I might as well get into one for trespassin' in two. Anyway, this is Mr. Redditch's garden an' he's gone away so *he* can't come out an' say we're torcherin' his cat. I chose it for hidin' in 'cause I knew it was Mr. Redditch's an' I thought it'd be a good place with him bein' away. I didn't know there was such a jolly good tree in it as this one. Look at it! It's easier even than the one in ole Miss Hopkins' garden. . . .'

'Well, I think we've done enough for one day,' said Ginger.

'All right,' said William. 'You go home. I'm goin' to stay an' have a shot at it. I mayn't ever get such a good tree for practisin' tree-dwellin' in all the rest of my life.' He had already manipulated the lowest branch and his voice came muted through the leafage.

'No, I'll stay with you,' said Ginger resignedly as he

made ready to follow his leader.

In a few minutes they had reached a broad flattish branch near the top of the tree.

'Gosh, this is a smashing one,' said William. 'I bet it's more comfortable than lots of ordin'ry beds. I——'

'Someone's comin' in at the gate,' said Ginger in an urgent whisper.

William peered through the branches. A muffled figure had entered the gate and was making its way in the shadow of the bushes towards the house. Though dusk was falling, William plainly recognised the pursed, pallid features of Mr. Redditch.

'Gosh!' he whispered apprehensively, but Mr. Redditch, his face lowered, his shoulders hunched, had passed safely beneath the tree.

Then began so strange a performance that William nearly lost his balance from sheer amazement. For Mr. Redditch approached the window of his house and, taking from his pocket a largish implement wrapped in a cloth, deliberately broke one of the panes, put his hand through the broken glass and slipped back the catch. He gave a stifled exclamation as he did so and they saw him take out his handkerchief and wrap it round his hand. Then slowly he raised the window and lifted one leg over the sill, catching his raincoat on a nail of the trellis fixed to the wall and tearing a hole in the lining. He gave another stifled exclamation—this time of annoyance—clutched the coat about him, lifted the other leg over the sill and vanished from sight.

'What's he doin'?' said Ginger. 'I thought he'd gone away.'

'I 'spect he's come back for somethin' an' forgotten his key,' said William. 'I bet I could have found a way in for him if he'd asked me. What's he doin' now? Can you see?'

They edged their way along the branch and craned their necks till they could see through the window. And there a yet stranger sight met their eyes. For Mr. Redditch was opening drawers and cupboards and strewing their contents on the floor till the carpet was almost hidden by them.

'Crumbs!' said William. 'The things grown-ups can do without gettin' into rows! I'd get into a row all right if I made all that mess in a room. He's not even put the drawers back . . . an' he's not found what he's lookin' for yet. An' he's goin' out of the room without even botherin' to clear it up.'

'Wonder what it is he's forgotten,' said Ginger.

'P'raps it's his camera. P'raps he wants to take some snapshots on his holiday same as people do an' he's left his camera behind an' so he had to come back for it.'

'Or it might be his pyjamas.'

'Or his money.'

'Or his fountain pen.'

'Or his watch.'

'Or his lighter.'

'Or his bath sponge,' said Ginger a little feebly.

At this point their imagination flagged and they turned their attention to the house again.

'There he is!' said William excitedly as a figure quickly passed an upstairs window. 'He's not found it yet.'

'*Might* be his bath sponge,' said Ginger, who felt that this suggestion needed a little bolstering up. 'He might want a bath after his journey and find he'd forgot his sponge an' it might be early closin' day where he's gone to so he couldn't buy another so he's had to come back for it.'

'An' forgot his key.'

'Yes.'

'Look! He's come downstairs again. He's in the dining-room now. Let's get on that next branch an' see what he's doin'.'

They removed themselves to the next branch and the manoeuvre was rewarded by another strange spectacle, for

Mr. Redditch was revealed in the act of taking an assortment of silver from a cupboard and packing it carefully into a suitcase.

'Fancy comin' all the way back for that!' said Ginger.

'P'raps it's his birthday tomorrow an' he wants to have a party,' suggested William. 'Grown-up people always want to use posh things at parties. They haven't any *sense* at all....' His eyes wandered round the room and widened still further in surprise. For there, too, drawers and cupboards had been opened and their contents tossed on to the floor. 'Well, I'm glad he's found what he came back for, but I never saw anyone make such a muddle lookin' for anythin' before. Gosh! I wish my mother could see it. She'd never call *me* untidy again.'

'I bet she would,' said Ginger.

Mr. Redditch, throwing a last glance round the room, was making his way out of it. They waited expectantly for his reappearance at door or window but nothing happened. He could not be seen at any of the windows. He did not emerge from the front door.

'I b'lieve he's in the back garden,' whispered William. 'I b'lieve I heard somethin'.... Come on. Let's have a look.'

They climbed down the tree and crept round the corner of the house ... to witness the most mysterious happenings of the whole mysterious evening. For Mr. Redditch was engaged in digging a hole in his vegetable patch between a row of runner beans and a row of celery. Having dug the hole, he put the suitcase into it and covered it with soil. Then he dug another hole and, taking a pair of shoes from his pocket, proceeded to bury them, covering them over with soil and carefully forking over the surface of the surrounding soil to hide all traces of his cache. Then he put the fork into the tool-shed and made his way furtively round the side of the house, past the rhododendron bush behind which the boys had taken cover and out again into the road.

William and Ginger emerged from the bush and stared at each other.

'*Well!*' said Ginger. 'What did he do that for?'

William considered. There were few situations that William could not explain to his own—if to no one else's—satisfaction.

'I bet I know,' he said. 'They're valu'ble things an' when he went on this holiday he got worried 'case someone stole them so he thought he'd come back an' hide them an' he did, but he'd forgot his key so he had to break a window.'

Ginger considered this.

'Funny place to hide 'em,' he said at last.

'Y-yes,' agreed William. 'They'll get jolly wet if it rains. But I s'pose he thought thieves'd never think of diggin' up a garden. It was jolly clever in a way.'

'What about his shoes? Why did he bury his shoes?'

'Well ... p'raps he was fond of them an' didn't want them to get stolen. P'raps he'd gone mountaineerin' in them. People *do* get fond of boots an' shoes they do things in. Robert makes an awful fuss about his rugger boots an' so does Ethel about the boots she's got her skates on.'

'I s'pose so,' said Ginger vaguely. He looked round at the gathering dusk. 'I guess it's about bed time. We'd better go home.'

But William found it difficult to leave the place. Its fascination lay strong on him.

'Let's jus' have another look through the windows at all the muddle he's made,' he said.

They went round to the front of the house and, looking in through the windows, feasted their eyes on the open drawers and cupboards and the littered carpets.

'Crumbs!' said William. 'I bet his mother would have somethin' to say to him if he'd got one. I wonder if he's left the upstairs rooms as bad.'

'We can't see the upstairs rooms,' said Ginger, 'so we don't know.'

William's eye roved round and came to rest on a trellis to which a rose tree clung half-heartedly.

'I bet I could get up an' have a look,' he said. 'After all that tree climbin' I've done a bit of trellis is nothin' to me.'

'Well, don't start tryin' to be a trellis-dweller,' said Ginger, chuckling at his own wit.

'Now watch me,' said William putting a foot in one of the trellis holes and swinging himself up.

His progress was slow. He was encumbered by rose shoots, scratched by thorns and hampered by the narrow footing the trellis holes afforded but at last he gave a cry of triumph.

'I can see right into it now an'—an'—Gosh! it's jus' as bad as the others. *Gosh!* It's worse. Everythin' all over the floor an'—an'——' His voice rose to a cry of 'Help!' as, with a harsh rending sound, the trellis collapsed beneath his weight and came crashing to the ground.

He crawled out of the *débris*—crowned with rose shoots, festooned with bits of broken trellis—and picked himself up.

'Well, *now* you've done it,' said Ginger, staring aghast at the destruction that surrounded them, 'an' he'll *know* it was us 'cause Miss Hopkins saw us come in an' she'll tell him. Huh!' He gave a good imitation of William's sarcastic laugh. 'That bow an' arrow an' fireworks took away's goin' to be nothin' to what's goin' to happen to us now.'

William removed some rose shoots from his hair and a piece of broken trellis from his foot, then stood for a few moments in an attitude of deep thought.

'*Tell* you what!' he said at last. 'If we could do somethin' to *help* Mr. Redditch he might be so grateful he wouldn't mind about the old trellis.'

'What could we do?' jeered Ginger. 'You tell me *one* thing we could do.'

'All right, I will,' said William. 'I've got a jolly good

idea. You know those things he dug into the garden to keep 'em in a safe place from thieves.'

'Yes?'

'Well, we could dig 'em up an' put them in a *really* safe place. That suitcase'll get ru'ned in the earth if it rains an' so will those shoes. If we dug 'em up an' hid 'em for him in my wardrobe at home instead, they'd be safer from thieves than in his garden *an*' they'd keep dry. Thieves might easy go diggin' about in his garden stealin' plants an' things an' find them. An' then when he comes home from his holiday we'll take 'em round to him dry an' safe, an' he'll be so grateful he won't say a word about the trellis . . . It's a jolly good idea, isn't it? Let's get the fork out and start.'

'I dunno that we ought. . . .' said Ginger.

'Oh, come *on*,' said William, who was already opening the door of the tool-shed.

A few minutes later they were making their way down the road, carrying the suitcase between them, their trail marked by pieces of damp earth that dripped from the suitcase and odds and ends of trellis and climbing rose that detached themselves at intervals from William's person.

They slackened their pace in a slightly apprehensive manner when they reached William's house, but fortune seemed at last to be on their side. No one was about. Unchallenged and unimpeded they went up to William's bedroom and hid suitcase and shoes at the bottom of William's wardrobe. It was not till they were coming downstairs again that they met Mrs. Brown in the hall.

'William!' she said. 'What a state you're in! Where *have* you been? It's *ages* past your bedtime. Your father's just come in and he says that if you aren't in bed by——'

She stopped. The two had vanished as at the wave of a magician's wand—William up to his bedroom and Ginger in the direction of his home.

The next morning William awoke to a confused memory

of a crowded and eventful day. William frequently awoke to confused memories of crowded and eventful days but he had a vague idea that this one was more crowded and eventful than usual. Sitting up in bed, frowning thoughtfully, he sorted out the events as best he could. The bow and arrow ... the rocket ... his father's wrath ... tree-dwelling in Miss Hopkins' garden ... tree-dwelling in Mr Redditch's garden ... the broken trellis ... the rescue of Mr. Redditch's goods.

He got out of bed and opened his wardrobe door.... Yes, the suitcase and shoes were still there. He would be able to hand them over, safe and dry, to Mr. Redditch on his return. So the broken trellis, at any rate, he thought optimistically, should not bring any complications in its train. There remained the tree-dwelling in Miss Hopkins' garden and the alleged torture of her cat.

He went downstairs and breakfasted heartily and in comparative silence, throwing wary glances at his father, who was, as usual, entrenched behind his newspaper. It was Saturday, so Mr. Brown would be at home all day. An announcement that he would not be going to golf made William's heart sink. He had been consoling himself by improbable mental pictures of Miss Hopkins coming to complain to his father, finding him at golf, going home and forgetting all about her grievance.

'What are you going to do this morning, William?' said his mother.

He hesitated. Wisdom urged him to absent himself as far and as long as he could from the scene of possible retribution. Curiosity urged him to stay near at hand and watch events. There had always been more curiosity than wisdom in William's make-up.

'I'll jus' be messin' about in the garden,' he said.

'Don't mess too much,' said Mrs. Brown with a smile, and Mr. Brown gave a sardonic snort from behind his newspaper.

The first part of the morning passed without incident. William occupied himself in making paper darts and testing their aerial flights, keeping a watchful eye upon the road. Then—things began to happen.

First of all Miss Hopkins appeared, bringing in her train an obviously reluctant Mr. Redditch. She had swept him up, ignored his protests and brought him along with her to demand an interview with Mr. Brown.

William waited for the summons. It came.

'William! Come in here at once.'

William entered the sitting-room by the french windows. His father stood on the hearth rug, the thunder clouds again upon his brow. Miss Hopkins and Mr. Redditch stood facing him.

'Torturing our cat up the tree!' Miss Hopkins was saying. 'Trespassing in our garden and torturing our cat up the tree! The poor thing was screaming with agony.'

'I wasn't torcherin' any ole cat,' said William indignantly. 'It was Ginger bein' a dog an' Ginger an' me bein' birds. They were jolly good birds an'——'

'Be quiet, William,' said Mr. Brown. 'You'll have an opportunity of giving what explanation you can later.'

Miss Hopkins, who had merely stopped to draw breath, continued:

'And, not content with trespassing in our garden, we saw him—*saw* him with our own *eyes*—go into Mr. Redditch's garden and start trespassing in that. I thought that Mr. Redditch was away——'

'I was away,' said Mr. Redditch, 'but the police phoned for me to come back early this morning. They had found the house broken into and ransacked by burglars. *Ransacked.*'

'But——'

'Be quiet, William.'

'Tinker hasn't been home all night. He's not up the tree now. I can't think *what*'s happened to him.'

'Ransacked from top to bottom. Smart work of the police. They noticed the broken window and got into touch with me at once.'

'Yes, but listen. I——'

'Be *quiet*, William.'

'We could hear the poor darling mewing for help up that tree while those cruel boys——'

'All my Georgian silver gone. Not a piece left. A most valuable collection.'

'Yes, but——'

'Will you be *quiet*, William!'

'Most unfortunate having to return like this the first day of my holiday.'

'The sweetest disposition. He wouldn't hurt a fly. How those cruel boys had the heart to——'

'But listen. I——'

'An expert's job, the police think. Fortunately the stuff was insured but the mess they made in the house has to be seen to be believed.'

'We've had him since he was a kitten. He's never had a harsh word, and to be *tortured* by those boys up a tree. . . .'

'If you'd jus' listen——'

'Be QUIET, William.'

'The police are there now looking for clues. I really oughtn't to have left the place, but Miss Hopkins insisted.'

'Of course I insisted.'

'A policeman's come, dear,' said Mrs. Brown in a resigned tone of voice, opening the door to admit a stalwart form in blue.

'S'cuse me interrupting,' said the policeman. He looked at Mr. Redditch. 'I heard you'd come here, sir, so I followed you.' He took a notebook from his pocket. 'I think I've got all particulars now. Footmarks on the garden bed just below the window. Shoes with distinctive pattern on rubber sole. Large size. Twelve or thereabouts.' Mr. Redditch glanced down at his own small, neat feet. 'Window broken, of course. That's what first drew our attention to the fact that the premises had been entered. Trellis broken down.'

'I don't understand about the trellis,' said Mr. Redditch with a puzzled expression, then stopped in confusion.

'Oh, that's quite simple, sir,' said the policeman. 'The thief intended to climb up to the bedroom window by the trellis and when it broke under his weight he smashed the downstairs window instead and slipped back the catch and got in that way. No finger marks, of course—they all wear gloves these days—but plenty of footmarks on the parquet flooring indoors. A large man, as I said, wearing shoes size twelve or thereabouts. You're insured, sir, I hope?'

'Yes,' said Mr. Redditch. 'Fortunately I'm insured.'

'Oh, dear!' said Mrs. Brown. 'Here's someone else coming to the door. I'll go and open it.'

'If you'd jus' *listen*——' began William again.

'William,' said Mr. Brown, 'once and for all, will you be *quiet*!'

Mrs. Brown re-entered, followed by a tall, keen-eyed young man.

'Good morning,' said the young man in a business-like tone of voice. 'I've just been to Mr. Redditch's house and was told that he was here.'

'Yes, there he is,' said William, 'an' if you'd jus' let me——'

'*William!*' said Mr. Brown.

'I represent the Mayflower Insurance Company,' said the young man, 'and, as I happened to be on a job over at Hadley, they asked me to come over and see you. I gather that you rang them up earlier this morning to report a theft.'

'Yes,' said Mr. Redditch. 'I've had some very valuable pieces of Georgian silver stolen.'

'I've got 'em,' said William. 'I've got 'em all. I've got his shoes, too.'

'William, be——' began Mr. Brown, then stopped. 'What did you say?'

'I've got 'em,' said William. 'I've got his shoes an' all those pieces of George silver upstairs in my wardrobe.'

'Don't talk such nonsense,' said Mr. Brown sternly.

'But I have,' persisted William. 'I've been tryin' to tell you an' you wouldn't listen. Me an' Ginger were bein' tree-dwellers in Mr. Redditch's garden las' night an' we saw him come back an' break his window 'cause he'd forgot his key. He cut his hand doin' it.' Mr. Redditch hastily tried to conceal the long red cut on his right hand. 'An' he tore the inside of his raincoat, too.' Mr. Redditch made a movement as if to clutch his raincoat about him, but the man from the insurance company whipped it open, exposing a jagged, three-cornered tear. 'Well, then he packed up these George silver things in a case an' buried 'em in the garden so they'd be safe from thieves an' he buried his shoes, too, 'cause he used to go mountaineerin' in them an' he didn't want them stole, an' Ginger an' me broke the trellis so we thought we'd dig up his George stuff an' shoes an' put 'em in a place where they wouldn't get wet if it rained an' then we thought he wouldn't mind about his trellis if he found we'd kept his George stuff an' shoes safe an' dry for him.'

'Will you stop talking this arrant nonsense!' thundered Mr. Brown.

'A pack of fantastic rubbish!' sputtered Mr. Redditch.

'One minute, one minute, one minute!' said the man from the insurance company. 'You say you've actually *got* the things, my boy?'

'Yes, an' I'll *show* you,' said William.

He plunged upstairs and plunged down again, holding the muddy suitcase in one hand and a pair of muddy shoes in the other. He opened the suitcase and poured a stream of silver on to the hearth rug. They stared at it, open-mouthed.

'There!' he said to Mr. Redditch. 'It's all there. We've

78

'There,' said William. 'It's all there!'

saved it for you—Ginger an' me. It rained las' night an' it might have got *soaked* if Ginger an' me hadn't saved it for you, so I bet you feel grateful to us an' won't mind about the trellis now, will you?'

The look that Mr. Redditch turned on William expressed many things, but gratitude was not among them.

'This is your silver, Mr. Redditch?' said the man from the insurance company.

'Yes,' said Mr. Redditch.

'And the shoes?'

The man from the insurance company was examining the shoes. They were large—size twelve or thereabouts—and they had rubber soles marked in a distinctive fashion.

'They're them,' said the policeman.

Mr. Redditch turned a putty-coloured face to him.

'I don't know anything about them,' he muttered.

'Strange!' said the man from the insurance thoughtfully. 'Well, I take it you won't be making a claim now.'

Miss Hopkins, who was standing by the window, gave a sudden scream.

'There's my darling Tinker!' she said.

A large grey cat could be seen ambling in an airy fashion down the road, with tail erect.

She rushed out of the house and returned holding the fiercely protesting animal.

'There's the wretched boy, my darling,' she said, pointing at William. 'Oh, if my Tinker could *speak*!'

Her Tinker struggled out of her grasp, jumped on to the floor and went to William, purring and rubbing itself against his shoes.

'I don't think he'd have much to say, if he could,' said Mr. Brown dryly.

In the diversion caused by Tinker's return, Mr. Redditch had made a quiet and unobtrusive exit, bundling silver and shoes unceremoniously into his suitcase. The policeman followed. Miss Hopkins also followed, holding

the struggling Tinker in her arms and cooing at him affectionately.

Mrs. Brown drew a deep breath.

'*Well!*' she said. 'I think I'll make a cup of coffee.'

'You see,' the man from the insurance company explained to William, stirring his coffee thoughtfully, 'this
chap staged a burglary because he wanted to get the insurance money. I suppose he'd have put in a pretty stiff
claim and then—as likely as not—he would have sold the
stuff as well. Do you understand?'

'Yes,' said William, adding zestfully (for William liked
his drama laid on thick), 'He's prob'ly the head of a gang
of international crim'nals. Prob'ly Scotland Yard have been
huntin' for him for years. He's prob'ly a smuggler as well.
An' a spy. He's prob'ly foiled the best brains in the Secret
Service.'

'Well, hardly that, I think,' said the man from the insurance company mildly, 'but the fact remains that you
happen to have saved my company a tidy sum of money
and I think that I can safely say that if there's anything in
particular that you'd like as a reward we'd be willing to
give it to you—within reasonable limits, of course.'

William threw a wary glance at his father, then turned a
wooden, expressionless face to the man from the insurance
company.

'I'd like a bow an' arrow an' a box of fireworks, please,'
he said.

'Oh, William!' said Mrs. Brown reproachfully. 'You
know your father said——'

But Mr. Brown waved the objection aside. The thunder-
clouds had cleared from his brow. Life stretched before
him again, free and unhampered. No longer would Mr.
Redditch poison his game of golf, shatter the peace of his
morning journey to town, play havoc with his gardening
implements. He even had a shrewd suspicion that Mr.

Redditch would soon be leaving the neighbourhood altogether.

'No, no, no, my dear,' he said genially. 'That's quite all right. Quite all right. As Ginger aptly put it, circumstances alter cases.'

CHAPTER IV

William and One of Those Things

'LOOK at it!' said William, gazing at the small toy aeroplane in the shop window. 'An' only two bob!'

'It's a Gloster Meteor,' said Ginger, pressing his nose against the glass.

'Or a Vulcan.'

'Or a Hunter.'

'Or a Swift.'

'Anyway, it's wizard. We could have a Farnborough display with it.'

'Yes,' agreed William, 'if we'd got two bob, but we haven't. I haven't any money at all, have you?'

'No.'

William considered deeply for some moments, then said:

'Didn't you say you'd got to take your aunt's cat to the vet's this afternoon?'

'Yes,' said Ginger. 'It's had something wrong with its ear. It's all right now, but she wants me to take it to the vet's so's he can *say* it's all right. She's bats on it.'

'Well, p'r'aps she'll give you a tip for takin' it,' said William.

'An' p'r'aps she won't,' said Ginger bitterly. 'She's never given me a tip for anythin' yet an' she's not likely to start today.' He, too, considered deeply for a few moments then went on, 'It's a long time since Robert gave you a tip.'

'Y-yes,' agreed William.

His thoughts went to his elder brother Robert, who was in his eyes the incarnation of tyranny, unreasonableness, ruthlessness and vindictiveness. On the other hand there was no denying that Robert had his better moments.

'He can't kill you,' encouraged Ginger.

'Can't he!' said William darkly. 'He nearly can. He nearly did that time I tried to mend the silencer on his motor-bike for him. I'd got it to pieces all right an' I bet I'd have got it together again all right if he'd let me go on with it. I'd taken out the thing that was makin' too much noise. At least I think I had.'

'Well, you've not done anythin' to make him mad lately, have you?'

'No, but someone else may have done somethin' to make him mad an' that comes to the same thing.'

'Well, let's try, anyway.'

'All right,' said William doubtfully. They began to walk slowly down the road. 'I bet it won't come off. It's a funny thing but I never seem to catch anyone in a good temper when I want them to give me money. It seems as if some-thin' sort of *told* them I was goin' to ask them, so's they could get in a bad temper ready for it. Anyway, I don't know where he is. He went off to tennis an' I bet he won't be home yet an'——'

'There he is!' said Ginger.

Robert was just coming round the bend of the road, accompanied by a slender girl with blonde hair and eyes of periwinkle blue. They were evidently returning from the tennis club. Robert was in white flannels and the girl in a white tennis slip that was obviously inspired by Wimbledon but owed not a little to the art of home dressmaking.

'Gosh!' said William. 'He's with that awful Roxana Lytton.'

'Well, he ought to be in a good temper, then,' said Ginger. 'He's bats on her, isn't he?'

'Yes, but she's not bats on him now. She used to be, but she's met someone called Osbert an' she's bats on him now instead.'

It was clear that all was not well with the couple. Roxana's perfect mouth was set in lines of petulance, and Robert's countenance was overcast.

William hesitated.

'P'r'aps I'd better not——' he began.

'Oh, go on,' said Ginger. 'Have a shot at it anyway.'

Impelled by his friend, William stumbled into the track of the approaching couple.

'What on *earth*——?' said Robert, pulling himself up and directing an angry gaze at his young brother. 'What do you mean by barging into us like that? Have you no manners? Have you no——'

'Listen, Robert,' interrupted William desperately. 'It's only two bob an' it's wizard an' if it isn't a Gloster Meteor it's jolly like one ... An' listen, Robert. I'll do everything you want me to all the rest of my life if you'll——'

'Get out of the way,' said Robert wrathfully, 'or I'll——'

William hastily removed himself from the path of the couple and they passed on down the road.

Roxana's petulant voice floated back to them.

'It's so *maddening*. Daddy's done everything he could and she won't even *listen*. It isn't as if she wanted the ground.'

'What's she talkin' about?' said Ginger.

'Oh, I remember now,' said William vaguely. 'I heard Robert talkin' about it at home. They want to make a tennis court—Roxana's family does—an' they want to buy that bit of land at the bottom of the Botts' orchard that sticks out into their garden an' Mrs. Bott won't sell it to them.'

'Gosh! The things they find to make a fuss about!' said Ginger in a tone of mystification. 'It's a rotten game, tennis, anyway. Jus' hittin' a ball over a net. You can't even get a goal in it.'

William was gazing back at Robert and Roxana.

'I 'spect she's goin' on an' on' an' on at him,' he said. 'Well, it serves him right for not givin' us that two bob.'

William was right. Roxana was going on and on and on, and Robert's face grew each moment more harassed and troubled.

'It's so *mean* of her. Daddy's written and telephoned and been to see her and she just gets ruder and ruder. He wanted to have the tennis court ready for my twenty-first birthday and it's just awful of her not to let us have it. He doesn't mind what he pays but she just won't sell it. She's —well, I won't soil my tongue with what she is.'

'I'm terribly sorry,' said Robert.

Roxana gave her golden head an angry toss.

'That's what everyone says but no one *does* anything.'

'There doesn't seem anything one can do,' said Robert.

'Oh, yes,' said Roxana sarcastically. 'That's what everyone says, too. When I think of the number of friends I thought I had, who said they'd do anything for me—*anything*—and the way that, now I'm in desperate trouble and need help, they all leave me in the lurch'—she sighed— 'except Osbert.'

'Osbert?' challenged Robert aggressively. 'What can Osbert do?'

It was Osbert—a dim youth with a man-of-the-world manner and a car of excessively contemporary design— who had ousted Robert from his position as Roxana's favoured suitor. She gave him the special smile that she

85

had once kept for Robert. She went for drives with him. She asked him to tea. She held with him those long confidential discussions about nothing in particular that she used to hold with Robert. And Robert, expelled from his paradise, could only watch and gnash his teeth.

'He hasn't decided yet,' said Roxana with dignity, 'but he's thinking out a plan, which is more than you're doing.'

Robert began a snort of amused contempt, then checked it midway and decided to make a last desperate effort to re-establish the old relations with the beloved.

'Don't worry, Roxana,' he said tenderly. 'I expect it will sort itself out. Things do sort themselves out. I've been in lots of jams myself and they've generally—well, sorted themselves out . . . Listen, Roxana, there's a new road-house just beyond that village that you liked when we went through it last month. You said it would look sweet done in colours on a Christmas calendar, you remember. It wouldn't have occurred to me because I'm not artistic like you, but I felt it was a beautiful thought . . . Well, I wondered if you'd care to go out there on my motor-bike next Saturday and have tea there. . . .'

'I'm sorry,' said Roxana distantly. 'I'm going out with Osbert in his car next Saturday.'

'Oh . . .' said Robert. 'Well, you won't forget that you're going to the tennis club dance with me, will you?'

Roxana raised delicate eyebrows.

'The tennis club dance?' she said. 'I'm sorry, Robert. You must have misunderstood me. I've arranged to go to that with Osbert.'

'Osbert!' groaned Robert.

'Well, you see, Robert,' said Roxana sweetly, 'Osbert's the only one of my friends who's standing by me in this dreadful crisis. As I told you, he's thinking out a plan. He doesn't just—throw me aside like an old glove as the rest of you do.'

'If there's anything Osbert Sanderstead can do,' said

Robert savagely, 'I can do it. And I'll *do* it, too. I won't just talk about it like that braying jackass.'

Roxana drew herself up.

'How dare you speak of my friends like that, Robert!' she said. 'I don't wish to hear another word from you. I——' Curiosity got the better of her indignation. 'What could you do, anyway?'

'I could go to that Bott woman,' said Robert impulsively, 'and tell her what I think of her ... and I *will* go to her, too. I—I'll insist that she lets you have the ground. She needs a *man* to deal with her. I—I won't let her get away with it. Once she has me to deal with, she'll—she'll change her tune.'

Roxana stared at him, half impressed, half incredulous.

'Well, Daddy's been at her over and over again. I don't know what you've got that Daddy hasn't.'

Robert tried to think of something he'd got that Daddy hadn't and finally gave up the attempt. Incredulity was beginning to possess him, too, and the spurt of resentment that had prompted his rash offer was dying down. Mrs. Bott was a formidable opponent. Few people joined issue with her and came away victorious.

'You're going to her now, are you?' said Roxana, torn between hope and despair.

'I don't know about this very moment,' said Robert with a mirthless smile. They had reached the lane that led to Roxana's house. 'I—I'll just see you home first.'

'No, don't trouble to do that, Robert. Osbert's coming to tea and he'll probably be there waiting for me. You'd better go straight on to Mrs. Bott's, hadn't you?'

'Well—er—yes,' said Robert, giving a hunted glance around. 'Yes, I suppose I had. She—she may be out, of course.'

'You can wait till she comes in, can't you? ... Well, I must hurry on now. I don't want to keep Osbert waiting. Good-bye.'

'Good-bye,' said Robert in a hollow voice.

He stood hesitating for a moment or two, then adjusted his collar and with set stern face started off in the direction of the Hall. He walked slowly up the drive, stopping occasionally as if to admire the nondescript clumps of shrubs that bordered it. Reaching the front door, he drew a deep breath then raised the knocker and let it fall lightly back in a way that, with luck, might fail to attract the attention of the inmates. A housemaid came to the door. He assumed an air of hauteur.

'I wish to speak to Mrs. Bott,' he said. 'Urgently. On private business.'

The housemaid vanished, and, after a short interval, re-appeared.

'Mrs. Bott will see you in the morning-room,' she said, with a hauteur that almost equalled Robert's.

Robert went into the morning-room.

He emerged some moments later with a heightened colour and made his way hastily down the drive, throwing an occasional glance over his shoulder as if fearful of pursuit.

The interview had been a short one and in the course of it Mrs. Bott had disposed of him with a few brief, trenchant words. She had called him an interfering jackanapes, an impudent puppy, a nincompoop and, for no particular reason, a two-faced snake in the grass. She had said that she wouldn't sell that bit of land now for all the tea in China and had added that she'd put the police on him if he as much as showed his nose inside her house again. She had ended the interview by advancing upon him with so threatening an aspect that he had turned and fled from her in ignominious panic.

She stood now at the morning-room window, watching his departure. She was still breathing heavily, but there was a faint look of satisfaction on her plump little face. It had been a relief to unload on Robert some of the resentment that she felt against life in general. For Mrs. Bott, like Robert, was labouring under a sense of grievance. . . .

Ever since her husband had invented a sauce whose sales had raised her from the wife of a small grocer to the mistress of the Hall she had longed to get among what she called the 'high-ups', but the 'high-ups' ignored her overtures with a bland politeness that baffled her at every turn. There were times when she accepted this state of things. There were times when she rebelled against it and returned to the fray.

She had lately returned to the fray. Hearing that on the committee of the Women's Guild there were—in addition to the Honourable Mrs. Everton-Massinger, the secretary —three ladies of title and the mother-in-law of a bishop, she had joined the Guild, contributed lavishly to its funds, provided magnificent teas for all its meetings . . . and still, after two months' intensive effort, had not been asked to sit on the committee. It was, she was beginning to feel, more than flesh and blood could stand, and Robert, proffering his ill-timed request, had borne the full brunt of her anger.

Her plump little face a deep purple colour, she made her way to the library—a spacious book-lined room where Mr. Bott rested after meals and did his football pools.

'That there Robert Brown,' she burst out stormily as she entered, 'pokin' his nose into that there bit o' land at the bottom of the orchard! What's it got to do with 'im, anyway? *Him*.' Mrs. Bott was apt to drop her aitches but generally managed to pick them up again before they had gone too far. 'That there bit o' land belongs to us an' we're not selling it, not to no one, an' I told the saucy young 'ound so straight. *H*ound.'

Mr. Bott looked up from his football pool.

'We could easy let it go, love,' he said mildly.

'Not while I'm alive, we won't,' said Mrs. Bott with an ominous ring to her voice. 'If they think they can treat me like dirt, buying land off us whenever they've a mind to, they've got to think again. *Use* me, that's what they do.

Make a mug of me. Same as that there Women's Guild. I'm good enough to give 'em tea and find money for 'em, but ham I good enough to go on their committees an' suchlike? Ho, no!'

Mr. Bott gazed sadly at the podgy little figure of his wife. He did not share her passion for high life, but he was deeply attached to her and suffered with her in all her disappointments.

'In the swim, that's what you've got to be to get in with 'em,' she said, her voice sinking to a doleful note, 'an' I don't seem to be able to get in the swim no'ow, 'owever 'ard I try. *H*ard.'

'You do your best, love,' said Mr. Bott soothingly.

'Flower arrangements an' budgerigars,' said Mrs. Bott. 'That's what they're all goin' for now. They go to classes in Flower Arrangements an' they've got budgerigars what talk and if you don't do none of them there things you're not in the swim.'

'Well, you've been to a Flower Arrangement class,' said Mr. Bott.

Mrs. Bott was silent, thinking of the hour she had spent at a Flower Arrangement class, when such words as Design, Balance, Scale, Symbolism, Focal Interest, Rhythm, Fillers and Dominants had floated meaninglessly over her bewildered head.

'Yes, but I couldn't make 'ead nor tail of it, Botty,' she said at last. '*H*ead. I can do a nice vase of sweet peas an' gypsophila as good as anyone. Proper dainty, they look, but they don't seem to want 'em dainty no longer. I sent one in to their competition an' they didn't as much as look at it.'

Mr. Bott sought for some crumb of comfort to offer her.

'Well, you got a budgerigar, love.'

'Yes, but it won't talk, Botty,' wailed his wife. 'Theirs talk. They say "Polly, put the kettle on", an' "Ta-ra-ra-ra-boom-de-ay", an' "Good old Winny" an' things like that.'

'Well, you've got to 'ave patience, love. You've only 'ad it a week.'

'Yes, but I've been on an' on at it with "Pop Goes the Weasel" day in day out ever since it came an' it won't say a word. Jus' sits an' looks down its nose at me same as all the rest of 'em.'

She sighed, then a faint ray of consolation seemed to shine through her despondency.

'Anyway, I've took the stuffing out of that there Robert Brown,' she said.

She had certainly taken the stuffing out of Robert. He was standing in the garden, hands in pockets, gaze bent gloomily on the ground. He had failed in his mission. He had lost Roxana. The obnoxious Osbert had probably by now devised some cunning plan by which he could lay the fateful piece of land at Roxana's feet and win her lasting gratitude. There was, Robert felt, nothing left in life worth living for. It was just as he had reached this conclusion that William appeared at the garden gate. He had paid the toy shop another visit and made the shopman a sporting offer to weed his garden, polish his car, clean his windows and wash down his front door step in exchange for the aeroplane—only to be summarily ejected from the shop before he had had time to add the further offer, which had just occurred to him, of cleaning his chimneys.

He watched Robert's sagging figure for a few moments; then, on an impulse and feeling that, after all, he had nothing to lose, decided to approach him again. He approached him warily, keeping at a safe distance, poised ready for flight.

'I say, Robert!' he said. 'If you could jus' let me have two bob ...'

Robert turned a lack-lustre eye on him. His mind was still so busy plumbing the depths of despair that he didn't take in the full meaning of what was happening. Someone was demanding two bob from him. Absently he brought out

91

half a crown from his pocket and placed it in the grubby outstretched palm.

'Gosh!' said William faintly. '*Gosh*, Robert! Thanks awfully. I'll give you the change when I've got it.'

'Keep the change,' said Robert wearily.

What did wealth matter, what did anything matter, now that he had lost Roxana and his life was blighted for ever?

William walked away in a sort of dream. He couldn't believe it. Nothing like this had ever happened to him before. So deeply was he impressed by it that his sense of gratitude to Robert drove out every other emotion. He didn't even want to go and buy the aeroplane. He only wanted to relieve his mind of its burden of obligation. Robert was plainly in trouble and the source of the trouble was, William knew, the piece of land at the bottom of Mrs. Bott's orchard. William, an inveterate trespasser on other people's property, was familiar with the piece of land. It was a sort of promontory, jutting out into the garden of Roxana's father, that no one had ever bothered to cultivate, that was not indeed worth cultivating. Weeds flourished in it shoulder high. Bindweed romped blithely from end to end of it. Thistles raised their heads in it exultantly. Seedlings from the neighbouring trees made miniature forests in it. He and Ginger had once tried to play Cowboys and Indians in it and had had to give up the attempt.

It was outrageous, thought William, that Robert's peace of mind should be shattered by a bit of ground that you couldn't even play Cowboys and Indians in. He must do something about it. He—the idea came to him quite suddenly—he would go to Mrs. Bott and reason with her. He would put Robert's case before her and plead the justice of his cause. His memory of previous interviews with Mrs. Bott was not encouraging, but William's optimism was proof against discouraging memories. He would do it at once.

Arriving breathless and panting at the front door of the

Hall, he put all the pent-up force of his resolution into his attack on the large iron knocker.

The housemaid who answered his knock fixed him with a coldly disparaging eye.

'D'you want to break the door down?' she said.

'No,' replied William. 'I want to speak to Mrs. Bott. It's somethin' very important what can't wait.'

'Another of 'em,' said the housemaid with a shrug. She assumed her air of hauteur. 'What name shall I say?'

William eyed her suspiciously.

'It's William Brown, if you don't know,' he said, 'an' I bet you do.'

'I'd be deaf and blind in this here village if I didn't,' agreed the housemaid as she vanished into the recesses of the stately hall.

'She'll see you in the morning-room,' she said when she returned, 'and wipe your shoes and pull up your socks and tidy yourself up a bit and try to look a bit less like something out of a loony bin.'

'All right, all right, all right,' said William. 'You should know what they look like.' He performed a hasty toilet by running his fingers through his hair and wiping his face with something that passed for a handkerchief. 'Will I do now?'

'You'd *do* for anyone.' She took him by the ear and led him across the hall to a closed door. Then opening the door and dropping her left eyelid at William she announced resonantly:

'Master William Brown.'

Mrs. Bott, standing by the chimney-piece, received her visitor with an icy stare.

'Well?' she said. 'What d'you want?'

William paused for a moment, then plunged headlong into his recital.

'It's only two bob,' he said, 'an' I bet it's a Gloster Meteor an' Robert gave me two an' six an' they want the

93

tennis court for her twenty-first birthday an' he said keep the change an' you wouldn't miss it an' no one's ever let me keep the change before an' you've got a great huge garden without it an' I feel jolly grateful 'cause we hadn't any money at all an' now we can buy monster humbugs as well as the aeroplane an'——' He paused for breath.

'What are you talking about?' said Mrs. Bott tersely.

'That bit of land that Roxana's father wants to buy off you.'

Mrs. Bott looked at him for a moment in silence. She was still purple-faced and breathing heavily, but she had brunted the edge of her indignation in the interview with Robert. Her spirit was not broken, but it was showing signs of strain. Although she was as determined as ever not to sell the piece of land, she was beginning to search for reasons to justify her attitude.

'They ought to be ashamed of themselves, using a child like you,' she temporised.

'They're not usin' me,' said William. 'They don't know I've come. And'—indignantly—'I'm not a child. Gosh! I shall be twelve next birthday.'

'Now listen to me, William Brown,' said Mrs. Bott. 'That there bit of land's no use for nothin'—not for a tennis court nor nothin' else. It didn't seem to fit in with the orchard, so we left it an' there it's been year after year, full of weeds. *Cluttered* with weeds, it is. You couldn't get them there weeds out, not with a bulldozer, you couldn't. So you can just keep your finger out of this pie, William Brown, an' I don't know what I'm doin' wastin' my time on a whipper-snapper like you. So clear out.'

Her fighting spirit had returned. The light of battle gleamed in her eye. William cleared out.

But he was not a boy to abandon a project at the first set-back. His brow was drawn into a thoughtful frown as he walked down the drive. She had said that she wouldn't sell the land because it was full of weeds. The remedy was

94

simple. He would clear it of weeds. He would clear it of weeds and then she wouldn't have a leg to stand on. She'd *have* to sell it to Roxana's father if he cleared it of weeds. A mental vision of the almost impenetrable jungle damped his ardour for a moment but only for a moment. He would get Ginger to help him. Together they would make short work of it. He would fetch Ginger now and——

He had reached the gate and, glancing down the road, he saw Ginger walking towards him, carrying his aunt's cat. It was an ancient, somnolent cat of rusty black that allowed itself to be carried anywhere by anyone without interest or protest. It generally spent the day sleeping in Ginger's aunt's armchair, awakening only to partake of the large and appetising meals that Ginger's aunt prepared for it at regular intervals.

'I've taken it to the vet,' said Ginger, 'an' its ear's all right an' she's not goin' to give me a tip for takin' it. I knew she wouldn't.'

'Well, come on quick,' said William. 'Never mind the ole cat. Robert's given me half a crown so we've got to weed that bit of land at the bottom of Mrs. Bott's orchard so's she'll sell it to Roxana's father. We'll soon pull 'em up an' we'll get some monster humbugs as well as the aeroplane.'

Ginger considered this with a perplexed frown.

'I'd better take the cat back to my aunt's first,' he said.

'No, we can't wait for you to do that,' said William impatiently. 'We've got to clear those weeds out quick. Bring the ole cat along with you. It won't run away. It never does.'

'All right,' said Ginger, following William to the weed-infested piece of ground at the bottom of the orchard.

'Gosh! There's a lot of them,' he said, peering about him through a tangle of thistle and willow-herb.

'They pull up easy,' William assured him, dragging a handful up by the roots. 'We'll just go on pulling an' 'pullin' till there's none left, then she'll *have* to sell it.'

They worked in silence for some moments, then Ginger spoke in a quick warning voice.

'I say, William. Look! There's a gard'ner over there cutting the hedge an' he's seen us.'

The gardener had certainly seen them. He was staring at them grimly, menacingly. Then, with an air of purpose, he laid down his shears and began slowly to make his way towards them.

'Come on, quick!' said William.

Flight to the road was barred by the gardener's advancing figure. The only way left open to them was through the orchard towards the garden and house.

'Hi!' shouted the gardener, speeding his slow steps to a run.

'He's comin' after us,' panted Ginger.

'Hi!' shouted the gardener again, beginning to run still faster.

They fled through the orchard to the lawn and dodged behind one of the herbaceous borders. William still clutched his handful of weeds. Ginger had discarded his weeds but still carried the large black cat, who remained unmoved and unperturbed by the adventure.

'Quick! Into the shrub'ry!' panted William.

They plunged into the shrubbery. The gardener plunged after them. They dodged round the shrubs. The gardener dodged after them. A small lawn separated the shrubbery from an open french window of the house.

'Come on! Quick!' gasped William and, followed by Ginger, darted across the plot of grass through the open window and into Mrs. Bott's drawing-room.

The room was empty except for the budgerigar, who drooped in his cage on a small mahogany cupboard near the fireplace.

William and Ginger looked out of the window from the

cover of the curtains. The gardener was still searching the shrubbery.

'Well, we've thrown him off all right,' said William. 'We'll jus' wait here till he's tired of looking for us an' then we'll——'

He stopped. The sound of Mrs. Bott's voice and another voice sounded in the distance . . . growing nearer . . . nearer . . . It was clear that Mrs. Bott was bringing a visitor across the hall towards the drawing-room. William threw a desperate glance out of the window. The gardener had left the shrubbery and was standing in the middle of the plot of grass, gazing suspiciously at the house. The voices of Mrs. Bott and her visitor were almost at the door. There appeared to him to be no means of escape . . . till his eyes lit on a vast tallboy that stood against the wall.

'We could jus' squeeze behind that,' he said.

'Not with this cat, I couldn't,' said Ginger, 'And not with those weeds, you couldn't.'

'Well, let's bung them anywhere,' said William. 'I bet she won't notice.'

His glance shot round the room again. On a table by the window was a large empty ornamental plant pot. He thrust his handful of weeds into it, snatched the cat from Ginger's arms, opened the cupboard beneath the budgerigar's cage, flung the cat inside and, followed by Ginger, scraped his solid person painfully between the tallboy and the wall. They were only just in time. The moment the last of their persons had disappeared from view, the door opened and Mrs. Bott entered, accompanied by the Honourable Mrs. Everton-Massinger.

Mrs. Bott was in the library with her husband, recovering from her interview with William, when she saw the Honourable Mrs. Everton-Massinger coming up the drive.

'I bet she's coming to ask for something, Botty,' she said dismally. 'It's all they ever does—ask me for things.'

And the prophecy proved correct.

Mrs. Everton-Massinger was tall and thin with small, tight features and an air of bright intensity. Her shabby tweeds held a vague suggestion of county and the rest of her more than a vague suggestion of art-and-craftiness, committee meetings and the platforms of village halls.

She greeted Mr. and Mrs. Bott, threw a pained glance at Mr. Bott's football pool form, and came at once to the purpose of her visit.

'I wonder if you'd be so good as to help us out again, Mrs. Bott,' she said in her nasal, high-pitched voice. 'We're having a joint garden meeting with the Hadley Women's Guild next month. A pity it falls in the month when Lady Barnham will be away but it's just one of those things . . .'

'Yes,' said Mrs. Bott.

She tried to sound cold and dignified but she could only sound wistful and dejected.

'We wondered whether you'd be so good as to see to the teas again. The Young Wives would have helped us, but they're having an outing to Margate that day. Such a pity, but—well, it's just one of those things.'

'Yes,' said Mrs. Bott again.

'So, if we may count on you . . .'

'Yes, I'll see to it,' said Mrs. Bott with a touch of bitterness in her voice. 'I generally does, don't I?'

'So good of you,' said Mrs. Everton-Massinger with mechanical graciousness. 'I'm not sure what we shall do if it's wet.'

A light sprang suddenly into Mrs. Bott's face.

'You could 'ave it in my drawing-room,' she said eagerly. 'P'r'aps you'd like to come and see my drawing-room. I've just had all the chairs re-up'olstered. It looks a treat. *H*olstered.'

'Well . . .' said Mrs. Everton-Massinger without enthusiasm.

She evidently had no consuming desire to see Mrs.

A sleepy 'Miaow' came from the budgerigar's cage ...

Bott's drawing-room. But Mrs. Bott had a consuming desire to show it to her.

'This way,' she said.

Mr. Bott raised his eyes from his football pool form, his pencil poised over Arsenal, and sighed as his wife and her visitor left the room.

Their progress to the drawing-room was slow. Mrs. Bott had to stop at the window and point out the extensiveness of the grounds, had to stop at the magnificent hall wardrobe and display its elaborate fittings, had to stop at a large gilt-framed oil-painting and explain, 'It's a real old master. 'Olbein or Landseer, I forget which. I get a bit muddled. Holbein. Cost Botty a pretty penny, anyway.'

The visitor's manner became more and more distant and depression settled again over Mrs. Bott's spirit.

'An' this 'ere's the drawing-room,' she said, throwing open the door.

Mrs. Everton-Massinger glanced coldly round the large, ornate, over-furnished room.

'Not at all suitable for our little gathering, I'm afraid,' she said.

Then her eyes lit on the weeds that William had thrust into the plant pot and a gleam came into them.

'Oh, Mrs. Bott!' she said. 'What a wonderful Arrangement!'

Mrs. Bott gaped but Mrs. Everton-Massinger had crossed the room to the plant pot and was examining it, her hands clasped, her whole thin body quivering with ecstasy.

'The *composition*! ... The *line* of that groundsel and yarrow! ... The *rhythm* of the nettles and willow herb! It's wonderful! *Wonderful!* ... That seeded hemlock in the middle is an inspiration ... And that ragwort to complete the balance! Wonderful! ... And—— Oh, Mrs. Bott! The marvellous touch of *symbolism* in putting that seeded foxglove close to the one in bloom! And—oh, those thistles are so just right to give the sweep, the range, the compass. Oh, the originality, the *rightness* of the whole thing!'

Mrs. Bott had grown pale. She was opening and closing her mouth with fish-like motions. But at that moment a sleepy 'miaow' sounded from the direction of the budgerigar's cage.

The visitor swung round.

'Your budgie! ... But, Mrs. Bott, what a *marvellous* cat imitation!'

Again a sleepy 'miaow' came from—as it seemed—the budgerigar's cage.

'How *did* you teach it to miaow like that, Mrs. Bott? It might be a real cat! How long have you had it?'

'About a week,' said Mrs. Bott, rallying her scattered forces.

'Could it speak at all when you got it?'

'No,' said Mrs. Bott.

'And you've taught it to miaow like that in this short time?' said Mrs. Everton-Massinger. Her voice became more nasal and high-pitched than ever. 'Oh, it's marvellous.' Another 'miaow' sounded, still sleepy but on a rising note of protest. '*Marvellous!* I've worked on mine for months and even now it can only say "Rule Britannia", and so indistinctly that several of my friends say they don't recognise the words at all. This wonderful cat imitation in less than a week...' She sighed and shrugged. 'Oh, well, it's just one of those things....'

She looked at the plant pot, the budgerigar's cage and then at Mrs. Bott. There was a new respect in her eyes, a note almost of humility in her voice as she went on:

'I wonder if you'd consider coming on to the committee, Mrs. Bott. There happens to be a vacancy and if I propose you and Lady Barnham seconds you—as I'm quite sure she will—there'll be no doubt at all of your election.'

Mrs. Bott gaped, blinked, gulped and gasped.

'Oo, thank you,' she said. 'Thank you ever so.'

'And now I'm afraid I must be going,' said Mrs. Everton-Massinger.

Still gaping, blinking, gulping, gasping, Mrs. Bott led her visitor from the room.

As soon as the door had closed on them, the two boys crept out from behind the tallboy, dragged the sleepily protesting cat from the cupboard and made their way through the french windows across the now unguarded lawn, down the drive to the gate. Mrs. Everton-Massinger passed them at the gate. Her thin face wore a look of surprise and bewilderment.

'They talked a lot of nonsense, didn't they?' said Ginger as they stood watching the departing figure. 'I couldn't make out what they were talkin' about, could you?'

'No. I couldn't hear what they said anyway,' said William. 'My ears were all squashed up between the wall and that big chest of drawers thing. . . . Anyway, we can't do any more weedin' now. That ole gardener'll be on the lookout for us. Let's take the cat to your aunt's an' then go an' buy the aeroplane.'

'Yes, let's,' said Ginger. 'I say, we were jolly lucky old Mrs. Bott didn't find us in that room. I thought that cat'd given us away once, didn't you?'

'Yes . . . She'd have half murdered us if she'd found us,' said William. 'She's in an awful temper today.'

But Mrs. Bott was not in an awful temper. She was standing by her husband, gazing down at him, a blissful smile on her plump little face.

'I'm *on*, Botty,' she was saying triumphantly. 'I'm on that there committee at last.'

'I'm glad, love,' said Mr. Bott, folding up his football pool form and putting it into an envelope. 'What made 'em put you on?'

'The drawing-room. . . . Flowers in a vase an' that there budgerigar startin' to talk. It said "miaow" plain as plain.'

'Well I never!' said Mr. Bott. 'Thought you was tryin' to teach it "Pop Goes the Weasel".'

'Yes, I was, but it started off on "miaow" all of its own accord. . . . An', Botty, I feel that happy, I want to make someone else 'appy, too. *H*appy. I'll let 'em have that piece of ground. I'm not goin' to ring up that Lytton man after all the things he's said to me. I'll ring up Robert Brown an' he can tell 'em.'

'That's a good idea, love,' said Mr. Bott, affixing a stamp to his football-pool form envelope. 'He'll be grateful.'

'He was grateful all right,' said Mrs. Bott when she returned from her telephone conversation with Robert, 'but he seemed in a bit of a hurry.'

Robert was now engaged in telephoning Roxana, beaming ecstatically into the instrument.

'I've been to see Mrs. Bott, Roxana darling,' he was saying, 'and she's willing to let you have that piece of ground.'

'Oh, *Robert*!' gasped Roxana. 'How did you manage it?'

'Oh, I—er—I just put it to her,' said Robert nonchalantly. 'I just put your point of view to her. I—well, I made her see reason in the end. She didn't decide on the spot. She took a little time to think it over, but she's just rung me up to say that she's thought it over and that she'll agree to it.'

'Oh, Robert, you're wonderful,' said the dulcet voice at the other end of the wire. 'Simply wonderful! And all the time you were *acting* that wretched Osbert was just dithering. I've *taxed* him with it, Robert, and he had to admit that he hadn't got a plan at all. He hadn't even started thinking one out. I was furious. . . . Robert, I'd love to go with you to that road-house place on Saturday . . . and, Robert, it's all right about the tennis club dance.'

'Oh, Roxana!' said Robert. 'May I—may I come over and see you?'

'Yes, *do*, Robert. I've sent Osbert away. I couldn't stand him a moment longer.'

Hurrying out of the gate, his mind busy with a hasty reconstruction of his interview with Mrs. Bott, he collided with William and Ginger. Their cheeks bulged with monster humbugs and their heads were bent over a small toy aeroplane that their imaginations had already transformed into the star turn of a Farnborough display.

'Oh, take yourselves and your wretched contraption out of the way,' said Robert impatiently.

The mellowness that misfortune had shed over his spirit had vanished. It had regained its usual toughness.

'Gosh!' said William, picking up the happily uninjured aeroplane and turning to watch his brother's hurried progress down the road. 'Everyone seems mad today. Robert's mad an' Mrs. Bott was mad . . .' He looked at the chimneys of the Hall that could be seen over the trees and chuckled. 'I bet she's madder than ever if she's found those weeds in that pot. She mus' have found 'em by now, too. I'd like to hear what she's sayin'.'

'It won't do it no more, Botty,' Mrs. Bott was saying in a tone of mystification. 'Did it as plain as plain when she was there an' now it jus' won't do it.'

'Well, it can't go on miaowing all day, love,' said Mr. Bott. 'It's got to have a bit of a rest sometimes. I shouldn't worry about it.'

'I'm not worrying about it, Botty, but'—a thoughtful look came into her face—'there was somethin' a bit *queer* about the whole thing.'

' 'Ow d'you mean, queer?' said her husband.

'Well, you know, I don't remember *doin'* that there flower arrangement at all. Not a single blessed mem'ry of it, I 'aven't got. I *must* 'ave done it 'cause there it was, plain as the nose on your face. *H*ave. I must 'ave done it in a sort of trance.'

'Yes, you might 'ave,' agreed Mr. Bott.

'Or'—with vague memories of a lecture on psychology that she had once attended in the Village Hall—''me subconscious may 'ave done it, Botty, without me knowin' anything about it.'

'It might 'ave,' agreed Mr. Bott.

The thoughtful look had deepened on Mrs. Bott's face.

'An' there's somethin' else that's queer about it, too, Botty.'

'Yes?' said Mr. Bott.

'You know that tallboy in the drawing-room?'

'Yes, love?'

'Well, you know it's got four legs, two at each end ... Well, I got a sort of idea this afternoon that it had eight.'

'*Eight?*' said Mr. Bott, startled.

'Yes. Two at each end and four in the middle against the wall. Mind you, I never looked at it *straight*. I was that took up by what she was saying that I only sort of saw it out of the corner of my eye, so to speak, but I've got a sort of mem'ry of it standing there with eight legs.'

'Not eight,' said Mr. Bott firmly. He could swallow the trance and the subconscious, but he couldn't swallow the tallboy with eight legs. 'Not eight, it couldn't have had. Not the tallboy. You must have been mistook.'

'I expect I was,' said Mrs. Bott. 'Oh, well——' She sighed and her voice unconsciously took on a high-pitched nasal accent as she continued, 'I suppose it's just one of them there things.'

'That's it, love,' said Mr. Bott reassuringly. 'It's just one o' them there things.'

CHAPTER V

William and the Old Boy

WILLIAM walked slowly along the road, his hands in his pockets, his toes dragging through the dust, his eyes fixed on the ground in a thoughtful frown.

He was on his way home from a particularly painful interview with the headmaster (the result of a series of unsatisfactory reports from Mr. French, William's form master) and was solacing himself with various daydreams suitable to the occasion. The most satisfactory was one in which the headmaster came to him in a state of abject terror, explaining that he had committed a crime, that the police were on his tracks and begging William to give him shelter and find him a hiding place. He implored forgiveness for all his unkindness and pleaded for help.

'You're the only boy in the school I can count on,' he said. 'As soon as I heard that Scotland Yard was after me, I said to myself, "Brown's the boy to go to. Brown will know what to do. Brown will get me out of this scrape. Brown will forgive me all the wrong I've done him and save me from my dreadful fate. . . ." You will help me, won't you, Brown? I daren't trust myself to any other. You're the one boy in the school I can turn to.'

The abject, grovelling Mr. Marks was a pleasant picture to contemplate, and William contemplated it with pleasure, raising his drooping figure and beginning to swagger down the road.

Then he proceeded to rally and encourage the criminal.

'Yes, I'll forgive you,' he said magnanimously, 'but' (repeating, as far as he remembered them, the words the headmaster had used in the recent interview) 'I hope this'll

e a lesson to you and that you'll conduct yourself different
future. . . . An' come on. I know a place where I can hide
ou an' where no one'll find you an' I'll bring you food an'
ou can hide up there till it's all blown over.'

Mr. Marks stammered broken words of gratitude and
William led the cringing figure across the field in the
shelter of the hedge to the old barn.

'You'll be all right here,' he said. 'If Scotland Yard
omes after you jus' hide under those sacks in the corner.
've hid there lots of times an' no one's found me. Now I'll
o home for tea an' I'll come back with a bun or somethin'
or you.'

Nearing the gate of his house, William informed an
imaginary policeman that he had seen a man who might
ave been Mr. Marks going down the road in the direction
of the aerodrome and that he was probably by now in a
Comet on his way to France. He watched the policeman set
ff at a run in the direction of the aerodrome, and, smiling
riumphantly, entered his home.

A large plate of raspberry buns (freshly made by Mrs.
Brown) drove everything else from his mind for the first
ive minutes; then, the edge of his appetite blunted, his
houghts turned again to the picture of Mr. Marks, cower-
ng in a corner of the old barn. . . . He had promised him a
un. He slipped a bun into his pocket. The real and
imaginary often became so closely merged in William's
mind that he found it a little difficult to disentangle them.
He finished the last crumb of the last bun on the plate,
resisted the temptation to eat Mr. Marks's bun, and made
his way across the field to the old barn.

He entered it with a careless swagger, then stopped on
he threshold, open-mouthed with amazement. For Mr.
Marks was in the barn, not cowering in the corner but
standing in the middle, looking around him.

'Ah, Brown,' he said vaguely. 'Perhaps you can help me.'
He took a letter from his pocket. 'I've heard from James

Aloysius Worfield—an old boy of apparently unlimite
wealth—who is proposing to visit the school. He was be
fore my time, so I don't know him, but'—he turned over
page of the letter—'he hints that he would like to presen
the school with some tangible memorial of his visit.
pavilion for the playing fields is the idea that occurs to me
but I realise that the gentleman must be handled carefully
He says that he hopes to find the landmarks of his boyhoo
unchanged. He gives a list of them and I thought I'd chec
up on them personally before answering the letter.' H
scanned the pages again. 'He mentions first the old barr
... This is the old barn, I presume?'

'Yes, but it's our place,' said William a little indig
nantly. 'We always play here.'

'Doubtless, my boy. Doubtless. But when you in you
turn are a prosperous city gentleman or an ornament t
some learned profession——'

'I'm going to be a diver, sir.'

'Yes, yes ... well, the particular sphere on which yo
shed lustre by your presence does not affect the situation
Other boys will still play here and regard it as thei
property.'

'Yes, I suppose so, sir,' said William, surprised and
little outraged by the idea.

'The old barn, then, I may tick off.... Perhaps you ca
help me with the others.' He consulted the letter again
'The tree with the hole in its trunk in Crown Woods....'

'Yes, sir. That's still there.'

'The ruined cottage with the apple trees down in th
valley....'

'Yes, sir.'

'The stepping stones over the river....'

'Yes, sir.'

Mr. Marks folded up his letter.

'That's all right, then. I can tell the gentleman that hi
landmarks still stand.... I'm not looking forward to hi

visit. He sounds a typical example of the class of moneyed Old Boy—a class I find particularly tiresome. However, one should not say such things, so we'll consider it unsaid. Now don't let me keep you from your business, whatever it is. By the way, what did you come for?'

'I came to bring you a bun,' said William.

'That was kind of you,' said Mr. Marks mildly. 'How did you know I'd be here?'

'I hid you here,' said William. 'I mean, you'd got into trouble with the p'lice an' you came—I mean, I sort of pretended you came—an' said you were sorry about this afternoon an' asked me to hide you an' put the p'lice off an' I hid you here an' told the p'lice you'd gone to the Cont'nent an' I was bringin' you a bun to stop you starving.'

'This afternoon?' said Mr. Marks. Beneath his professional assumption of dignity, he was an absentminded and kind-hearted man. He had already forgotten his recent interview with William, but a moment's thought recalled it to his mind. 'Ah, yes.... Yes, I understand.... Well, I consider that you have dealt with me very generously, my boy. Very generously indeed.... In similar circumstances in my own boyhood, I used to hold a court-martial and condemn the criminal to unspeakable tortures. I had a particular aversion to the science master, I remember, and I used to keep him hanging by his feet from the top of a pine tree for days on end.'

'That was a jolly good idea,' said William.

'You can have it for what it's worth,' said Mr. Marks absently. He looked at his watch. 'Well, I must be going on now....'

'Would you like your bun, sir?' said William, taking it out of his pocket.

Mr. Marks inspected it. Despite its sojourn in William's pocket, it was comparatively clean.

'Half will be sufficient,' he said. 'Perhaps less than half.'

'I'll eat the rest,' said William, dividing the bun and disposing of his own share of it in two large mouthfuls.

Then he stood in the doorway and watched Mr. Marks make his way across the field to the road, eating his bun in an absent-minded, meditative fashion.

Mr. James Aloysius Worfield arrived the next morning. Mr. Marks drove him from the station in his small, battered pre-war car, and later he addressed the assembled school. He was a large, stout, florid man with sleek black hair and an over-genial smile. In his address, which was long and rambling, he urged the virtues of 'sportsmanship' and 'cricket' and 'playing the game' and held up Mr. James Aloysius Worfield as a supreme example of these virtues.

'I was a little monkey, of course,' he said, flashing his expansive smile round the rows of bored listeners. 'I was full of mischief, up to any pranks, but I can honestly say that in all my years here I never did anything that was mean or underhand. . . .'

His audience listened with growing restiveness. Mr. Marks, sitting next the orator, rested his elbow on his knees and shaded his eyes with his hand as if to conceal his feelings under an appearance of deep thought.

The applause that greeted the end of the speech was due more to relief than to any appreciation of its sentiments.

'Rotten old show-off, wasn't he?' said William to Ginger.

But Ginger wasn't interested in Mr. James Aloysius Worfield. He was only interested in Mr. French.

'He's been worse than ever today,' he grumbled. 'Goin' on an' on' an' on at me. Took my caterpillar off me an' kept me in at break jus' for nothin'. Well, nearly for nothin'. . . . An' all those sarky things he kept sayin' to me. Gosh! I'm goin' to think of somethin' sarky to say back one of these days an' I'm jolly well goin' to say it.'

A sudden memory came to William's mind.

110

'Let's have a court-martial on him,' he said. 'Let's have a court-martial an' condemn him to—to unspeakable tortures.'

Ginger brightened.

'Yes, that's a good idea,' he said. 'When shall we have it?'

'We'll have it down by the river after afternoon school,' said William.

They chose a secluded spot on the river bank. A thick bush was chosen to represent the accused, and William and Ginger took up their positions facing it. William constituted himself president and Ginger chief witness.

William addressed the bush sternly.

'You're a crim'nal,' he said, 'an' you've got to be punished by lor. Did you or did you not steal a valu'ble caterpillar from this boy?'

The bush seemed to droop despondently.

'He did, didn't he?' said William, turning to Ginger.

'Aye, aye, sir,' said Ginger.

'You can't say "Aye, aye, sir", at a court-martial,' said William with a touch of irritation in his voice. 'You only say that on ships. You say, "Yes, me lud" at a court-martial.'

'Why?' said Ginger.

'Never mind why. Say it.'

'Yes, me lud,' said Ginger.

'You stole this valu'ble caterpillar off this boy,' said William, addressing the bush again, 'an'—an' you kept him imprisoned in the form room when he ought to've been out in the playground an' you—— What else did he do, Ginger?'

'He called me a congenial idiot,' said Ginger.

'Gosh! That's bad!' said William, shaking his head solemnly. 'Did he use those axshul words?'

'Aye, aye, me lud,' said Ginger. 'An' he said I'd got the brains of a cheese mite an' the manners of an orang-utan.'

'Well, there's nothin' wrong with orang-utans,' said William. 'I saw one in the zoo. It acted quite sensible.'

'If you're goin' to start bein' on his side——' said Ginger hotly.

'No, I'm not, I'm not,' William assured him hastily. He assumed a ferocious scowl and addressed the bush again. 'You're a crim'nal an' you've been proved guilty of stealin' valu'ble caterpillars an' keepin' boys imprisoned against the lor an' usin' bad language at them. Have you anythin' to say in your defence?'

The bush remained silent.

'I knew you hadn't an' I jolly well wouldn't listen if you had,' said William. 'I sentence you to——'

At this point a face appeared round the bush. It was a narrow, Puck-like face, with slanting, twinkling eyes, ruffled, greying hair and a long, humorous mouth.

'What's all this?' it said. 'A trial at law?'

'It's a court-martial,' said William coldly, 'an' it's private.'

'I'm sorry for intruding,' said the man, 'but it seemed to be almost over. What is the sentence going to be?'

'Well,' said William uncertainly—for his plans had not reached beyond the actual trial—'we might hang him by his feet from a tree.'

'No, no,' said the man. 'Too ordinary. Let the punishment fit the crime. He shall pick caterpillars off cabbages till not one remains in the purlieus of the village. He shall be on view in a cage at the zoo, fed on mite-infested cheese and jeered at by small boys through the bars.'

William chuckled.

'Yes, that's jolly good,' he said.

He peered around the bush in order to get a closer view of the originator of these suggestions. He saw a little man, wearing shorts and a shabby tweed jacket, sitting on the ground with a knapsack on the grass beside him.

'I was just going to have my tea,' said the man. 'Come

and join me. I have a lot of food to spare because I didn't stop for lunch. Just had a beer and a hunk of bread and cheese at a pub and pushed on.'

'Thanks awfully,' said William, as the two made their way round the bush. 'That's jolly decent of you.'

'Jolly decent,' said Ginger.

'Not at all,' said the man. He opened the knapsack and took out several large packages. 'The landlady who made up my packed meal this morning had liberal notions. There should be plenty.'

There was plenty ... sausage rolls, sandwiches, cake, apples, biscuits.

'Tuck into it,' said the man.

They tucked into it.

'Do you live here?' said William.

'No,' said the man. 'I'm doing a hiking tour. I think that October is the ideal month for hiking so I generally do one in October. This place doesn't really come into my itinerary but when I found that I was within a few miles of it, some impulse made me stretch a point and take it in. I was at school here, you see. You, I think'—he glanced at their ties—'now attend that particular educational establishment. ... All changed since my day, I expect. I took a look at it from the outside as I passed but I didn't go in. A mistake, I always think, to revisit one's old school in any capacity. The very expression Old Boy is revolting. But when I heard your court-martial I couldn't help being interested. It brought back the memory of a court-martial we held when I was at school.' He was silent for a few moments and his lips curved into a smile. 'Quite a story, that was.'

'Tell us,' said William through a mouthful of sausage roll.

The little man leant back and lit his pipe.

'Well, as I said, it's quite a story. ... We had a secret society. I expect you've had a secret society.' William nodded. 'About six of us. We all had secret names that no one else was supposed to know. All a dark secret. We met in a cave in the old quarry near Marleigh. A cave high up on the side of the quarry with a bush growing outside. . . . A pretty stiff climb to get to it, I can tell you. That was secret, too, of course, and we had a lot of hocus-pocus about it. Rules and oaths of secrecy and that sort of thing. One of the members was a boy whose secret society name was Porky. He had small eyes and little pointed ears like a pig. My name was Frisky, I remember, but I can't remember why. . . . An unpleasant sort of chap, Porky was, but he threw his weight about and did a lot of smarming up to people and somehow he took everyone in. Anyway, things began to vanish—money from pockets, penknives and oddments from desks and lockers. So we set a watch and we caught Porky at it. . . . Have a doughnut? They look good.'

'Thanks,' said William. 'They are, too.'

'It was a bit of a shock, of course, to find that the thief was a member of our secret society. Anyway, we had a meeting of the society the next day, court-martialled him and told him that he must sign a confession and we wouldn't report him to the Head unless he started his tricks again, in which case we would show the Head his confession. We turned him out of the secret society, of course. . . . Try one of those chocolate biscuits.'

'Thanks,' said Ginger.

'I've tried one,' said William. 'They're jolly good. I'll try another. What happened after that?'

The man gave a reminiscent chuckle.

'I remember Porky played one of his pleasant little tricks on me as we were climbing out of the cave. Came up behind me and tried to push me down the rock, but I saw him coming and stepped aside and over he went. Crack down on a rock. Cut his head open. Had to have half a dozen stitches in it and was in bed for over a week. Anyway, that was the end of the secret society.'

'Why was it the end?' said William.

'Well, the next day they started blasting in the quarry again and blasted away all that side of it. We could see the opening to our cave still high and dry with the bush still growing in front, but there was no way of getting up to it. Anyway, it was almost the end of the term and we were all leaving. We were boarders and I don't suppose any of us have been near the place since. I haven't till today when I found myself a couple of miles away from it and had a sudden fancy to come over.'

'This quarry . . .' said William thoughtfully.

'Now don't go messing about with the quarry,' said the man. 'It was dangerous enough in our day. It must be twice as dangerous now.'

'We know it . . .' said Ginger. 'It's on the road to Marleigh, isn't it?'

'A long time ago it seems now,' said the man ruminatively. 'It was hearing your court-martial that brought it all back to my mind. Your culprit was being tried in his absence, I gather. Who was he?'

'Old Frenchie,' said William.

'Our form master,' explained Ginger.

'Well, let him have it good and proper. Don't forget. Picking caterpillars off cabbages and stuck in a cage in the zoo. . . . And now you must run off or your parents will be wondering what's happened to you and I must be getting on. . . . Take what's left of the food.'

'*Thanks,*' said William and Ginger simultaneously.

'An' it's all been most int'restin',' added William.

The next morning Mr. French poured out his choicest sarcasms on William and Ginger, but they bore it unmoved, upheld by the pleasant vision of their tormentor laboriously removing caterpillars from cabbages and exhibiting his spindly person in a cage at the zoo.

Not only Mr. French but the whole staff seemed nervy and on edge. For Mr. James Aloysius Worfield was playing with Mr. Marks as a cat plays with a mouse. Sometimes he seemed about to present the new pavilion and sometimes he didn't. He obviously enjoyed the sense of power that the situation gave him. He didn't know. . . . He wasn't sure. . . . He had seen one boy surreptitiously reading a 'comic' when he was supposed to be studying Latin verbs, and he had seen another funking his opponent's right in a boxing match. Such things were not done in his day. They weren't cricket. They weren't playing the game. They weren't keeping a straight bat. Over and over again—to anyone who would listen to him and to many who wouldn't—he described the uprightness, the manliness, the sportsmanship, the pluck that had characterised his own boyhood. He described how he had acquired the scar that ran across his forehead in defending a 'little chap' against a 'bully' who then attacked him with a 'naked penknife'.

'And I never gave him away,' he would add with his fatuous smile. 'I had my faults, of course, but I was never a sneak.'

Mr. Marks wore a harassed, driven look. He was beginning to suspect that his visitor had thrown out his vague hints of a munificent 'memorial' merely in order to satisfy his self-importance and ensure his treatment as an honoured guest, without any real intention of fulfilling them. The entertainment of Mr. James Aloysius Worfield was an arduous task and one of which Mr. Marks and his whole staff were now heartily weary.

'Everyone's in a bad temper,' said William as he and Ginger made their way home from school. 'Thank goodness tomorrow's Saturday an' we needn't go to school.'

'Well, let's do somethin' excitin' tomorrow,' said Ginger 'Let's play Cowboys an' Indians.'

'No, let's go an' have a look at the ole quarry,' said William. 'It sounded jolly int'restin'.'

116

'It sounded jolly dangerous,' said Ginger.

'Well, I'm goin' anyway,' said William, 'an' you needn't come if you don't want to.'

'Oh, I'll come,' said Ginger resignedly.

A few minutes later they stood looking at the railed-off pit from which a few jagged rocks rose precipitously.

William's eyes were fixed on a rock that rose from the farther side of the quarry. Most of the lower part had been blasted away, but a bush clung precariously to the surface near the top.

'I bet that's the cave where they used to have their secret society meetings,' he said. 'I *bet* it is. There's the bush an' you can see a sort of a little opening behind it.'

'Yes, p'raps it is,' said Ginger, his eyes following the direction of William's finger. 'Well, we've seen it so let's go back an' play Cowboys an' Indians.'

'No, I'm goin' up to have a look at it,' said William.

'Gosh! You *can't*, William,' expostulated Ginger. 'You'd never get up there. It sort of hangs out all over the rest of it. There's no way of gettin' up to it.'

'Well, I'm goin' to have a try,' said William, 'an' you needn't come if you don't want to.'

'Oh, I'll come,' said Ginger again. 'It's goin' to be the dangerousest thing we've ever done in our lives, though. I bet the birds'll be pickin' our skeletons this time to-morrow.'

But William was already making his way to the bottom of the quarry.

'Well, we got down all right,' he said, rolling the last few yards between the rocks.

'Yes,' said Ginger, picking himself out of a small pool into which his descent had led him. He looked up at the jutting ledge. It seemed higher and more inaccessible than ever. 'Gosh, William, we'll *never* do it.... Listen. We've *seen* it. Let's—let's pretend that we've been into it.'

But William was already beginning the ascent, swinging

117

his sturdy form from ledge to ledge with the agility of a monkey. William was sure-footed and unimaginative. Heights did not disturb him. He had supreme confidence in his own prowess. Ginger acted on the simpler method of following William in blind confidence. He used the footholds and handholds that William had used, feeling them to be endowed with some sort of magic . . . and together—miraculously, as it seemed—the two swung themselves up on to the ledge, squeezed themselves behind the bush and through the little opening.

'Gosh!' panted William, looking round. 'It's wizard, isn't it!'

The cave, despite its narrow opening, was large and roomy, stretching far back into the rock. Its advantages as a meeting place for a secret society were obvious.

William's eyes roved round it with interest. Suddenly he gave a cry of excitement.

'Look!' he said. 'Here's their things!'

On a low ledge that had obviously been used as a table lay the evidence of the last meeting of the secret society before the final blasting of the quarry had cut off access to the cave. There were stubs of pencils, some mouldered remains of fruit, a dust-covered sheet of paper.

William took up the paper, blew away the dust and read:

'I, the undersigned, confess that I stole a shilling from Philips' pocket and a half a crown from Saunders' pocket and a penknife from Gregson's desk and a watch from Tillinson's locker and various other things at various times.'

The signature was 'Porky' with an indecipherable squiggle beneath it.

'Gosh! It's his confession,' he said.

'Let's bag the pencils,' said Ginger, 'an' here's quite a decent penknife. Well, it's only a *bit* rusty.'

'Here's a compass, too,' said William. 'They're jolly useful things to have, are compasses. They tell you where the North is ... an' here's an indiarubber.' He thrust the 'confession', together with a compass and indiarubber, into his pocket. 'They don't belong to anyone now so we might as well take 'em all.'

'It's goin' to be pretty awful gettin' down again,' said Ginger, peeping out of the narrow opening and drawing quickly back.

'No, it's not,' said William. 'It's goin' to be all right. We'll get down as easy as easy.'

This, perhaps, was unduly optimistic, but after a few hairbreadth escapes they arrived, battered, bruised, cut and shaken, at the bottom of the quarry.

'Well, that was jolly int'restin',' said William, picking himself up and carelessly examining a bleeding leg. 'I'm glad we did it. I wish we'd been there in those days an' could have belonged to it.'

'An' turned out ole Porky,' chuckled Ginger, removing some loose stones from his collar. 'I'm s'prised there's any skin left on my body.'

'Let's put ole Frenchie up there the next time we court-martial him,' said William. 'I bet he'd have a job gettin' down.'

'P'raps he won't be quite so sarky on Monday after pickin' off all those caterpillars,' chuckled Ginger.

But Frenchie was even more sarky on Monday and the nerves of the whole staff were more edgy than ever. For Mr. James Aloysius Worfield was still in residence, demanding constant attention, and still, apparently, he had not made up his mind about the pavilion. He was beginning to hedge even more openly, talking of the many calls on a man of his position, the erroneous idea of his wealth that seemed to have got abroad.

'I'd like to do something for the school, of course,' he said to Mr. Marks. 'That is, if I were a wealthier man and had not so many commitments already.'

The state of affairs had leaked out among the pupils. A bleak drizzle of rain and a dull mist lowered further the already dejected spirits of masters and boys.

'Wish I could think of somethin' to make him give that ole pavilion an' clear off home,' said William.

'I'm sick of hearin' him talk about cricket,' said Ginger.

'Gosh! That's an idea,' said William.

'What's an idea?'

'Cricket.'

'What d'you mean, cricket?'

'Well, it's cricket he's int'rested in. Straight bats an' things. He never talks about football. It's always cricket. He's sort of got cricket on the brain. ... If he could see us playin' cricket it might put him in a good temper an' he might give the ole pavilion an' go home.'

'Cricket!' expostulated Ginger. 'You can't play cricket in October. It's pourin' with rain an' the ground's all muddy.'

William waved the objection aside.

'You can play cricket any time,' he said loftily. 'You've only got to stick stumps in the ground an' throw a ball at them. Let's get Henry an' Douglas.'

The next morning Mr. James Aloysius Worfield, idly watching the boys at 'break' from the headmaster's window, was surprised to see four boys knocking stumps into the mud-swamped ground and proceeding to engage in what was evidently intended to be a game of cricket. He went down to investigate. He approached the players at the bottom of the playground. Ginger stood before the wicket, displaying an elaborately straight bat. William was preparing to bowl. Henry and Douglas stood in the attitude of expectant fielders.

'What on earth——?' began Mr. Worfield.

William delivered the ball.

He slipped in the mud in the act of delivering it and fell headlong.

The ball soared through the air and landed neatly on Mr. Worfield's brow.

Mr. Worfield in his turn staggered backward, slipped in the mud and fell headlong.

A titter arose from the watching boys.

Purple with rage, Mr. Worfield seized William by the collar and dragged him indoors to the headmaster's study.

'This boy,' he sputtered, 'has had the audacity to throw a ball at me. Deliberately throw a ball at me. I demand that he shall be instantly and severely punished.'

Mr. Marks looked at William's mud-covered countenance.

'I can't even see which boy it is,' he said. 'Wipe the mud off your face, boy.'

William delved into his pocket. He knew that somewhere beneath the accumulation of odds and ends there was a handkerchief. He found it and drew it out. The accumulation of odds and ends fell upon the carpet, among them a crumpled piece of paper with the words 'I, the undersigned...' and the signature 'Porky' plainly visible.

Mr. Worfield's eyes rested on it and a curious change took place in his countenance. The ruddy colour left his cheeks and an ashen hue invaded them. His eyes, fixed on the paper, bulged and grew bloodshot.

'Pick up that rubbish,' said Mr. Marks.

William picked up that rubbish. His gaze was fixed on Mr. Worfield.

Emotion had emphasised the peculiarities of Mr. Worfield's features—the small eyes, the pointed ears, the thick nose that resembled a snout. The jagged scar across his brow showed up sharply.

'Porky!' gasped William.

Mr. Marks looked at William in amazement and then, with increasing amazement, at Mr. Worfield. Beads of perspiration stood out on Mr. Worfield's brow and trickled down his face. His pallid lips were drawn back in a sickly smile.

'Come, come, come!' he said. 'Perhaps I was over hasty. Doubtless I was over hasty. I'm a hasty man. Impulsive, generous, courageous—but inclined to be hasty.' He took out his handkerchief and wiped the perspiration from his brow. 'Let me have a word with this boy alone, Headmaster.'

Mr. Marks shrugged his shoulders and left the room.

Mr. Worfield turned to William. The perspiration still glistened on his brow. The sickly smile was still plastered on his lips.

'Where did you find that piece of paper, my boy?' he said. 'The one that fell out of your pocket.'

'Oh, that!' said William. 'I found it in a cave in the old quarry.'

Mr. Worfield uttered a neighing sound that was evidently intended to be a laugh.

'I remember. I remember.... Some boys held secret society meetings up there. I wasn't a member myself, but I heard about it. I—er——'

A sudden idea had occurred to William. That indecipherable squiggle after the name 'Porky'.... He took out the paper and examined it.... It wasn't quite indecipherable, after all. Though hastily written and almost illegible, it still represented the words James Aloysius Worfield.

'It's got your name after "Porky",' he said. 'It's got James Aloysius Worfield.'

Mr. Worfield made a movement towards William. William made a movement towards the door, slipping the paper into his pocket. Mr. Worfield stood, reconsidering his tactics. The boy, though thick-set, looked active and nimble. He would dodge round the furniture. He would dart out of the door. The whole thing would be in the open.

'It's got your name after "Porky",' said William

Again he uttered the neighing sound.

'Yes, yes,' he said. 'I remember. We had a sort of game. We all wrote imaginary confessions. How it all comes back! One wet afternoon.... I've forgotten what I pretended I'd done.... Now you're a sensible boy. Let's do a deal. This bit of paper is of no use to you, but it will be of value to me—just as a little memento of my boyhood. It's useless to you, isn't it?'

William's school reports emphasised with monotonous regularity his lack of serious application to his studies, but he was not altogether devoid of intelligence. He turned a bland, expressionless face to his interlocutor.

'I think Mr. Marks'd sort of like it, too,' he said. 'He's got a sort of museum of old things about the school. I think he'd like this for his museum.'

Mr. Worfield moistened his dry lips.

'What nonsense!' he said. 'A mere paper game! What possible interest could it have for him? A paper game of imaginary confessions played on a wet afternoon.'

'But Frisky said ...'

A greenish hue spread over Mr. Worfield's face.

'You know Frisky?' he stammered.

'Oh, yes. I know Frisky,' said William.

Mr. Worfield abandoned finesse.

'How much will you take for it?' he said.

'Well,' said William thoughtfully, 'Mr. Marks sort of wants a pavilion for the playing field.'

'Of course, of course, my boy,' said Mr. Worfield, recovering something of his aplomb. 'I have every intention of giving one. That was one of my main objects in coming here.'

'Shower baths and changing rooms.'

'Of course, of course.'

William thought quickly.

'A holiday tomorrow.'

'Yes, yes, my boy,' said Mr. Worfield with the ghost o

his old geniality. 'All work and no play makes Jack a dull boy. Ha-ha!'

'An' me not gettin' in a row over that cricket ball, 'cause we thought you'd like it. Straight bats an' things.'

Mr. Worfield flinched.

'Exactly, exactly. Boys will be boys. I was one myself once. Ha-ha! And—er—I take it that this foolish little paper game will go no further? I mean, there might be people who wouldn't realise that it was only a game.'

'Yes, that's all right,' said William. 'I forget things jolly quick.'

Mr. Worfield met William's eye and somehow felt that he could trust him.

'Well . . .' he said, holding out his hand.

William placed his hand firmly over his pocket.

'Things are in a bit of a muddle in my pocket,' he said. 'I'll be gettin' 'em sorted out while you fix it up with Mr. Marks.'

Mr. Worfield threw him a glance of unwilling admiration as he went to the door.

Mr. Marks and Mr. French were talking together at the end of the corridor.

'Come along, Headmaster,' called Mr. Worfield. 'Our little interview is over.'

Mr. Marks looked curiously at his guest as he entered the study, followed by Mr. French. He was a strange and not a prepossessing spectacle. Red and green patches seemed to alternate on his face, his brow was still damp with perspiration and his thick lips were twitching nervously.

'Well, well, well,' he said, baring his teeth in a wolfish grin, 'we've had our little talk and I'm willing to overlook the whole thing . . . I—I ask that the boy has no further punishment.'

'As you wish,' said Mr. Marks.

'Your lucky day, Brown,' said Mr. French dryly.

Mr. Worfield took out his watch.

'I'm afraid that I must return this evening and I'd like to fix up that little affair of the pavilion with you, Headmaster, before I go.'

He drew a cheque book from his pocket and went to the desk. Mr. Marks and Mr. French followed him, staring with amazement at the figures he was writing on the cheque.

'It's extremely generous of you, Worfield,' said Mr. Marks. 'I'm most grateful.'

'Not at all, not at all,' said Mr. Worfield. 'That should cover all incidentals such as changing rooms, etcetera.'

Then they turned to William, who stood watching them impassively.

'What are you hanging about for, Brown?' said Mr. Marks, slipping the cheque into his wallet. 'Off with you!'

'What on earth has the boy got in his pockets?' said Mr. Worfield, neighing on a high-pitched note. 'Turn them out, boy . . . String, 'bus tickets, matchbox, bit of paper . . . The fire's the best place for all that junk.'

He threw the handful on to the flames, watched his 'confession' blacken into ashes, then drew a deep breath and mopped his brow again.

'G'bye,' said William politely as he turned to the door. Ginger was waiting for him at the gate.

'Told you it wouldn't work,' he said gloomily. 'What happened?'

'Oh, nothin' much,' said William vaguely. 'A bit of a mess-up but it ended all right. An' I've got some good news.'

'What?'

'There's goin' to be a holiday tomorrow. A whole holiday.'

'Good!' said Ginger. 'Let's play Cowboys and Indians.'

Mr. Marks and Mr. French stood by the window, looking at the taxi that was bearing their guest down the drive on its way to the station.

As it vanished from sight Mr. Marks took the cheque from his pocket and contemplated it with satisfaction.

'Well, we got it,' he said.

'We got it,' said Mr. French, 'in spite of young Brown.'

'In spite of young Brown,' agreed Mr. Marks. Then a thoughtful look came over his face. 'Or could it be—we shall never know, of course—could it possibly be *because* of young Brown?'

LOOK OUT!

Look out for the happy Pocket Merlin symbol when you're feeling like a few hours of real reading enjoyment. A paperback with the smiling wizard on the cover guarantees the very best in fiction. Whether you like adventure or fun, old favourites like William or Billy Bunter, or the very latest stories, the growing Merlin range will have something 'just for you'. If you have difficulty in getting hold of the book you want (and they sell out fast) just pop three shillings and the name of the book you want in the post and send it to The Hamlyn Group Ltd., Hamlyn House, The Centre, Feltham, Middlesex. (U.K. only)

There are over Fifty titles in the Merlin range now—and these are of special interest to all boys . . .

Richmal Crompton

William
William the Rebel
William the Gangster
William and the Space Animal
William and the Moon Rocket
Just William
William's Television Show
William the Conqueror

Reg Dixon

Pocomoto—Pony Express Rider
Pocomoto—Tenderfoot
Pocomoto and the Robber's Trail
Pocomoto and the Texas Rangers

Frank Richards

Billy Bunter's Big Top
Billy Bunter and the Secret Enemy
Billy Bunter and the Man from South America
Billy Bunter and the School Rebellion
Billy Bunter and the Crooked Captain
Billy Bunter's Convict
Billy Bunter and the Bank Robber
Billy Bunter—Sportsman!

Ted Cowan

The Shivering House

Robert Bateman

Cameraman

John Wingate, D.S.C.

Submariner Sinclair